ZANE

SUSIE MCIVER

ZANE

BAND OF NAVY SEALS

AUTHOR
SUSIE MCIVER

This is a work of fiction. Names, Characters, organizations, places, events, and incidents are either products of the author's imagination or are used fictitiously.

Text copyright 2021 Suise McIver

All rights reserved. No, part of this book may be reproduced, or stored in a retrieval system, or transmitted in any form or by any means, electronic, mechanical, photocopying, recording or otherwise, without express written permission of the author.

Cover Design by-Emmy Ellis

❀ Created with Vellum

1

ZANE

Damn, that woman's going to be the death of me. Why can't she be the elderly Aunt Polly I pictured in my mind?

Zane couldn't find Missy's aunt Polly anywhere. When he arrived in Tennessee, he went straight to the concert where Missy told him her aunt would be. Zane walked around checking every elderly woman standing up close to the stage, asking her if she was Polly Devlin. Missy had said her aunt was singing, so he assumed she was next to the singers. He had one of those elderly women grab him and plant a kiss on his lips. He was so shocked he stood there for a moment before taking her arms from around his neck. He took a step away from her as she took a deep drag from her cigarette. One woman told him Polly was on stage before she took a long drink from her whiskey bottle. Zane didn't pay any attention to her.

How the hell am I supposed to find one old woman in this mess of people? Missy said she came to see her friend Shay Darwin's concert. So she has to be here somewhere. He stopped walking as Shay told the crowd to welcome her friend Sugar on stage.

The crowd went wild as one of the hottest women Zane had ever seen walked on stage.

Zane stood there and watched as she smiled at the crowd, and then she began to sing. He felt like she was singing to him. It looked like her eyes were trained on him. Damn, he was already hard. How the hell did he let this happen? Zane had more control over his body than to let one gorgeous woman with a sexy as hell voice turn him on. Didn't he? *Fuck*, he guessed he didn't.

He pushed his way through the crowd, completely forgetting about Aunt Polly. He only had one mission on his mind, and that was reaching this woman. Her beautiful green eyes locked with his. She reminded him of someone, then it dawned on him who it was, Missy Devlin. Zane frowned as he watched her, so this had to be Polly Devlin. But it couldn't be. She was too young. Definitely no Aunt Polly. Secondly, she couldn't be so foolish. A damn hired killer was after her, and she stood on stage where anyone could take a shot at her.

Without thinking, he stepped on the stage as she finished her song. Zane took her hand and pulled her off the stage. Only, it wasn't that easy. Polly tried getting loose from him. Zane admitted he should have tried to explain who he was, but this woman had his mind and body doing things he wouldn't usually do. He was confronted by two men who were almost as big as him. They blocked his way. He put Polly behind him.

"Get the hell out of my way."

"Get your hands off of Miss Devlin. Or we'll take them off for you!" one of the men growled.

Zane smiled. Most people who knew him would have backed up when he smiled like that. Before they knew what he was about, he had used moves they didn't see coming, and all of a sudden both of them lay on the ground knocked out cold.

~

"Who the hell are you?" Polly asked, standing with her hands on her hips.

Zane smiled at her, and it almost melted her body where she stood. She spotted him when she sang her sexy new release. Polly couldn't move her eyes from his. For the first time in her life, she wanted a man at first sight. Polly could feel her panties getting wet. She wanted this man. Too bad she didn't have casual sex.

"Zane Taylor, I'm your bodyguard."

"These two are my bodyguards," she said, pointing to the men on the ground.

Zane raised an eyebrow, "You've got to be kidding. There is a hired killer who was paid money to kill you. Do these two look like they are guarding you? I think not. I'm with the Band of Navy Seals Security. Rowan has Missy, and I have you."

"You don't have me. So that was what Missy was calling me about—" she had a panic look come over her face. "Is Missy alright?"

"She is now. I'm surprised you left her alone. Someone broke into your house. Someone who Chester hired to kill her, he also hired someone to kill you. That's where I come in. You hired us to guard you and her, and that's what we are doing." He took her hand and pulled her along.

Polly dug in her heels. "Wait, we can't leave. I still have three more songs to sing."

"You are going to have to skip those songs."

"The hell I am."

"Look, Polly," Zane shook his head and chuckled, "I still

can't believe you're Missy's aunt. If you get on that stage, you are a sitting target. I can't watch you from the ground because I can't see who's watching you."

"Then you can be on the stage with me."

"Hell, no." There was no way Zane would make a fool of himself in front of all these screaming people. He could picture himself standing on stage hard as a rock while this beautiful woman sang. "Wait, damn it, don't you care for your life?"

"I know you will watch over me." Polly looked at the two guards sitting on the ground, "You two can pick your checks up." She turned and talked to a woman who was two feet from them, "Make their checks out and pay them for six months. Zane will be my bodyguard from now on."

Zane stared at the woman in the shadows. He didn't know she was there. He couldn't get a good look at her. He thought he heard her chuckle because she was able to walk upon them. How did he not hear her walk up behind him? Zane looked at her feet. She had moccasins on. Zane pulled her out of the shadows and smiled.

"What are you doing here?" he said, pulling her into a hug.

"I came to see my friend's sing. What are you doing here?"

"I'm Polly's bodyguard."

"Sorry, Dakota, I thought you were Mary. Do you two know each other?"

"Yes, we've known each other for years. Dakota, you are more beautiful every time I see you. Are you living on the reservation now?"

"I have been staying there with my uncle. He was going through chemotherapy. But he's doing so much better now. I'm trying to talk him into moving out to Skye's place. She has a small cabin out behind the horse barn that she's fixed up for him. He's pretty stubborn."

"I hope he moves there, you two are his only family now. Are you staying in Tennessee for a few days?"

"No, I'm going home tomorrow. Skye is expecting a baby any day now. So I'll be staying at her house for a month to help her out."

"Damn, doesn't she already have a ton of people living there?"

Dakota laughed, "No, most of the girls besides Julia have moved out. They have their own place now. Julia is hardly ever around. She does a lot of undercover stuff."

"I've seen her on a couple of her undercover jobs. When you see her, tell her I said she needs to start wearing a disguise. Julia is becoming well known as a heavy-drug dealer, but she doesn't try to hide her looks and that can turn dangerous. She could get herself killed. You may want to slip Skye that info. Well, I'm glad I got to see you. I better get on stage with Pollyanna."

"Why do you call her Pollyanna?"

"Because it's her name."

Dakota smiled and walked away as Zane climbed the steps to where Polly sang her heart out.

Polly wondered about Zane and Dakota. They seemed to be good friends. She was relieved when she saw him standing at the edge of the stage, looking out at all the people. Damn, he was one good-looking man. His suit didn't have a wrinkle on it. His tie was still straight even after he knocked out her bodyguards. Her next song was all about love and aching for love. Polly looked at Zane Taylor as he watched her. Without thinking about what she was doing, Polly walked over to where he was. She sang to him and him only. The crowd went wild.

Zane wondered what she was doing when she moved his hair off his forehead. Her body couldn't get any closer to his, with an audience watching. He wrapped his arm around her waist and pulled her closer still. He couldn't help himself, he wanted to strip her clothes off her and make hot, passionate love to her. She had no doubt how his body was reacting to hers. When she finished singing, they gazed into each other's eyes. Lost in the moment, Zane bent his head and kissed her. He wrapped both arms around her, and held her tightly against him. She gave back what he gave her. Zane ran his hands under the edge of her shirt and touched her skin. The watching crowd shouted as loud as they could. Shay came over and put her hand on Zane's shoulder, he didn't want to raise his head, but he knew he had to.

Polly didn't care how loud the people got. Her only concern was getting closer to Zane Taylor. She was on fire for him. When he raised his head reluctantly, she pulled him back to her. When he raised his head again, she moaned out loud. Polly slowly opened her eyes. She couldn't think. He kept a hold of her, or she would have fallen on her butt. Polly didn't want to move. She knew he wanted her as much as she wanted him. She felt it with every fiber in her body. Polly also felt it leaning against him. She didn't back away from Zane. She was leaving it up to him to take a step back. It dawned on her that Shay was singing, and she had to get over and sing her part. Stepping back, she took a breath to calm her racing heart. Polly turned the moment her part came up, and her voice was only a little shaky. The crowd went crazy. She heard Zane chuckle.

Zane, couldn't believe he lost track of where he was. My God, he would have to stay away from Pollyanna. She could make him lose his head, and Zane Taylor never lost his head.

Polly had never in her thirty-three years on earth kissed a stranger and loved it. *I don't even know the man. Hell, just because he's hot and smells so damn good doesn't mean you can kiss him the way you did. God, he did smell good.* Polly kept an eye on Zane as she sang. He stayed on stage and watched the people in the audience. He looked like he could stop anyone who got near her.

Polly and Shay sang another song. The crowd wanted more, so Polly sang one more before stepping back. They still wouldn't stop shouting. She looked behind her and knew what they wanted. She walked over to Zane and pulled him to the edge of the stage. Polly raised their hands, and Zane pulled her into his arms and kissed her. She was lost in the kiss when he raised his head. His eyes were half-closed, then he gave her another quick kiss.

Polly wanted to stamp her foot. She didn't know if it was because she wanted more or was angry at him for kissing her. She would put a stop to it the first chance she got.

Zane put his arm around her waist and tucked her into his side. Damn, he wanted this woman. Zane wanted her like he's never wanted a woman before. He glanced at her. Polly looked like she was mad as a wet hen. Zane smiled; he knew he was going to get an ear full soon. As soon as they were out of sight from the people, she moved his arm from around her.

"I don't know what you're used to with your other clients, but you will not kiss me again."

"Actually, it was you who kissed me first on stage. I knew what your audience wanted, so I gave it to them. Otherwise, they wouldn't stop shouting for more. I never kiss my clients. You're the first."

"Don't do it again."

"Be sure you tell yourself that as well."

Polly didn't know how to answer, so she raised her head high and walked past him to her dressing room. He walked in behind her. "No. You are not coming into my dressing room. I'm going to change my clothes. I have to show myself at a party tonight. I haven't shown myself at any of the others I've been invited to."

Zane leaned against the wall waiting for her to dress. He saw someone looking around the corner. He decided to check them out as soon as he had the chance. He heard the door open and stood straight. Polly was gorgeous with her long, wavy red hair and those beautiful green eyes. She had on a tight-fitting black dress that came to her knees and some white high heels. She almost was at eye level with him with her heels on. Zane was six-foot and two inches. He almost pulled her into his arms upon seeing her. Polly didn't wear much makeup; she didn't need it. "You're beautiful."

"Thank you."

"I saw someone looking around the corner. I'm going to check it out. Wait here for a second."

"There are always people who look around the corners here. Hurry up and check. I'm starving."

Zane was gone for two seconds; when he came back, Polly was surrounded by fans. He pushed his way to her and guided her away from them. "Sorry everyone, but Sugar is hungry, and we need to leave."

"Sugar, what are you going to order?" a fan called out.

Polly stopped and turned around, "I think I'm going to get fried chicken. I haven't had that in a while." She looked at Zane, "What about you Zane, what will you order?"

"Maybe a Mediterranean salad."

Polly made a face, "A salad, you only want a salad?"

"I might order some grilled fish if it's fresh."

Polly smiled as she watched Zane. He was broad across his shoulders. There was no doubt this guy was frigging sexy. "It was nice talking with you all. I'll be seeing you around." Polly waved as Zane guided her away from her fans.

. . .

Zane guided her through the halls and out the back door. "Where is your vehicle?"

"Right there," Polly said, pointing to a black SUV with a driver standing next to it. "And by the way, call me Polyanna or just Polly but never Sugar, that'smy stage name," she smiled at Zane but she was so stern that he wasn't sure how to take that. "Joe, let's stop at the Wagon Wheel and have dinner before we go to the party," She told her driver getting into the car.

"You got it, Sugar."

Zane smiled at her, "So Joe gets to call you Sugar."

"Yes," was all she said to him with a smirk. She turned to Joe,

"This is Zane Taylor; he's my bodyguard. Zane, this is Joe Phillips. He's my driver when I have concerts."

Zane nodded his head toward Joe. "Has anyone been hanging around the car?"

"Are you kidding me? I'm always chasing Sugar's fans away from her. They love her like the rest of us do but don't understand personal space."

"How do they know which vehicle she's in?"

"Because I'm always her driver."

Zane looked at Pollyanna sitting in the back with him. "That'll have to stop."

Polly turned her head and frowned, "Zane, you can't tell me who I hire to be my driver."

"While I'm your bodyguard, I'll tell you who will be your driver. I'll drive you myself after tonight."

Normally feisty, she couldn't find a quick response. Polly didn't want to sit this close to Zane. She could smell his scent, and all she wanted was to climb on him and have her way with him. *Damn it, stop thinking about his mouth and his hot body.* Polly turned her head away from him. She glanced at his hands as a memory came of him putting his hands under her shirt and touching her skin. Chills went through her body. She wanted to scoot closer to him. Finally, they stopped at the restaurant. Zane guided her into the restaurant with his hand on her lower back. Polly stopped and looked at him. "You don't have to guide me everywhere we go. So take your hand away from my hip."

Zane smiled, "Sorry, it's a habit I have when I'm with a beautiful woman."

"Are you always with beautiful women?"

"Most of the time, I am. I'll make sure it doesn't happen again."

For some reason, that answer didn't sit well with Polly. *I'm sure he does a lot more than touch their hips.* By the time their food arrived, Polly was so tired she could barely hold her eyes open. It didn't stop her from eating her food. She smiled at Zane as he ate his salad and grilled fish.

"I have a piece of chicken left if you want it," she said, smiling at him.

"Thank you, but I don't eat fried food."

"Not even French fries?"

"Nothing fried."

"Do you ever eat fast food?"

"I've eaten at some fast-food restaurants. Just not the fried foods."

"Have you ever eaten fried foods?"

"Why are you so interested in the food I eat?"

"I've never met a man who didn't like fried chicken or hamburgers."

"I eat grilled chicken and hamburgers. They aren't loaded down with grease that clogs your arteries."

Joe sat there eating his hamburger and fries. Not saying a

word. Zane smiled at Polly, and she smiled back. Joe could afford to lose an easy fifty pounds.

Joe wiped his mouth and grinned at both of them. "My wife would give me an ear full if she knew I was eating this now. My doctor said I need to stop eating fried foods but it's so hard to stay away from food this good."

"Joe, you shouldn't have ordered it then," Polly said, shaking her head. Then she burst out laughing. "Okay, let's get this over with and go to the party."

"You don't look like you want to go."

"Oh, Sugar doesn't enjoy parties much. Every time I drive her, she dreads it."

"It's not the party itself, it's the people. They drink too much and become annoying."

"What about Shay? She doesn't drink?"

"Shay is the only one that doesn't drink. She will stay forty-five minutes then sneak out the back way. Every time I try that, someone catches me."

"We're going to make sure we stay only an hour. Then I'll sneak both of us out," Zane said, gazing into her eyes.

Hell, did I just lean into him? "Great, I'm ready for bed." She could feel her face burning before she tried correcting herself. "I don't have to do another show until Friday in Houston."

They walked into the building. It was packed. "I'm pretty damn sure this is over the limit of people allowed in the building," Zane said, looking around. He saw a few people he knew, "Fuck, what is she doing here?" he let out.

"Who?" Polly asked, looking around.

"Look, Pollyanna, I'm going to have to say you're my girlfriend. I don't want Cheyenne to think she and I will end up together after the party."

"Why not tell her you are my bodyguard?"

"Because she won't care about that. Believe me, if you

aren't my girlfriend, she'll hang around until she can get me alone."

"I'm sure you are exaggerating."

"Zane, sweetheart, I didn't know you were in Tennessee. I've missed you so much." As Polly watched, the blond wrapped herself around Zane and kissed him. She took his arms and pulled them around her, and put them on her butt. As if she wanted him to push her closer to him.

Polly stood there and watched as Zane tried to untangle the woman from his body. She looked like a snake wrapped around him the way her arms and legs were.

"Excuse me," Polly said in a Southern drawl, "you have yourself wrapped around my man."

Zane chuckled, "Cheyenne, this is…"

"I know who this is. Hi Sugar, I always thought you didn't enjoy these parties."

"That was before I had Zane to come with me, but I'm sure we won't stay long, isn't that right, love," Polly said, pushing her way in between Zane and the snake, who still had her body pressed against his.

"That's right, darling, we'll say hello to some friends and leave." He pulled away from Cheyenne then stepped over to Polly and wrapped his arms around her. Then she surprised him by taking out a tissue and wiped his mouth off. She then dipped it into her glass of wine and wiped it again.

"I don't kiss anyone who has had another woman's lips on theirs. Especially since I know they'll be all over me tonight."

Cheyenne looked angry, then she shrugged her shoulders and walked away.

"Damn, I'm ready to take you home right now." Zane looked over Polly's shoulder, "Here she comes back," he lied, "we better let her know you meant what you said." He pulled her into his arms and devoured her lips.

Polly couldn't hear the people around her. All she knew

was the body taking whatever it could take from her, and she gave willingly. When Zane shifted to where she knew he wanted her, she pushed her body closer against his.

"You two do know you're at a party, right."

Zane didn't want to acknowledge the voice, but he had to. "Yes, we know. We are proving something to Cheyenne. "

"Yeah, I saw her here. I wondered if she saw you."

"What are you doing here, Jax?"

"See that beautiful blonde over there," he said, pointing at his sister, Susan, "I was visiting her, and she made me bring her here. I'm sure I'll be in at least three fights before the night is over. So why are you here?"

"I'm with my girlfriend," Zane looked at Polly, who looked like she wanted to kick him.

"Pollyanna, I would like to introduce you to my friend, Jax."

"Are you really his girlfriend?" Jax asked, grinning.

"No, I'm his client, and not for long if he kisses me again."

Zane put his hand over his heart. "You're breaking my heart, darling."

"If you're not careful, I'll break something else. One hour, then we leave. I'm going to talk to a few people."

"I'm going with you. I'll see you around, Jax."

"Zane, I'm serious. No more kissing. I don't care if Cheyenne strips you down to nothing and has her way with you. You are not kissing me again. I have a fiancé, and I'm sure he wouldn't like knowing my bodyguard keeps kissing me."

Zane frowned at her as she talked. "How come you never mentioned a fiancé before?"

"Why would I? We only just met. Secondly, you are my bodyguard. I don't need to tell you anything."

2

"So, tell me, how are things going with Aunt Polly?" Rowan asked Zane over the phone later that night. Then he laughed out loud. Polly had gone to bed, and Zane checked all the windows and doors to make sure everything was locked uptight.

"Did you know she wasn't an old lady, and I wouldn't be getting to bed by eight every night?"

"No, not until Missy showed us her photo."

"I asked Missy if her aunt was senile, and she said probably. That brat knew I was in for a surprise." Zane chuckled.

"That's why I'm calling. We saw the two of you kissing on stage. It's all over the news."

"There won't be any more of that. Pollyanna said she would get another bodyguard if I kiss her again. The only thing is she'll have to keep herself and her lips away from mine. She's the one who kissed me on stage. I'm telling you, Rowan, I've never wanted to get naked with anyone like I do this woman."

"Hurry and catch the guy who wants to kill her, then you

can leave Polly and her lips behind," Rowan laughed as he hung up the phone.

There were already surveillance cameras on the property and in the house. Zane laid back on the sofa with the camera screens on the television. He thought he could close his eyes for a minute. Zane jerked awake. *What the hell was that? He flew off the sofa and ran out the back door where the screaming was coming from.*

He saw Polly wrestling with a man by the pool. Zane charged the man. He lifted him up by the neck and threw him onto the brick wall. His fist hit the man in the face—three times before he stopped and took a step back. The guy was out cold. Zane looked around, and Pollyanna had a towel draped around her. She marched over to where he was and kicked the man twice before Zane pulled her away.

"Why the fuck did you leave the house without waking me? You could have told me you wanted to go swimming."

"It's my house. I'm supposed to be safe here!" she shouted. Then she began to cry.

Zane pulled her into his arms. He took his phone out and called the police. Zane tied the guy up until the law got there.

"This is the third time we've picked this guy up for harassing our country singers. We'll make sure he stays locked up this time."

Polly had taken a quick shower and dressed before coming back down. "If I see this bastard around my house again, I'm going to shoot the son of a bitch. Do I have to build a higher wall? It's already ten-foot-tall!"

"You should know this comes with being a singer," the policeman told her.

Zane was pissed. He knew how stalkers were. They became obsessed with the people they stalked. "So this isn't the one hired to kill you?"

"Are you saying she has a killer stalking her?" the policeman asked.

Polly looked over at him, "Don't worry about it. I go to Houston tomorrow. No one will know where I am."

"Are you kidding me? You have a concert in Houston. Everyone will know where you are! Zane exclaimed.

"We'll get a hold of you and let you know what's going on with this guy," the policeman told her.

Zane frowned. "How long are you going to be in Houston?"

"One night. Then I'm off to Dallas. Then I'm doing a charity concert in Brandon, Missouri. That'll be crazy because the people mingle with the singers. It never bothered me before, but I'm kind of uneasy now since that man attacked me."

"I'll be by your side the entire time. So you don't have to worry. Do you do concerts all the time?"

"If I want to stay in the top one hundred, I do. I have to put out new songs and do concerts. I do them about eight months out of the year. I also write songs for myself and others. So I stay busy. I hardly ever have a break."

"When do you go home?"

"I am home."

"I mean your house in Los Angeles?"

"That's Missy's home. I lived with her to help her out, but she's eighteen now. When my mother died, I lived with Missy for a few years. We came here when school was out. Then we went back to Los Angeles when school started back. If we would have stayed here, that fucking P.E teacher wouldn't have messed with her mind and had sex with her. If the neighbor hadn't stopped me, I would have killed him. That fucker took my niece's youth from her when he had sex with her. I hate him even if he is dead."

"Missy said it was your house."

"I gave it to her. I didn't need a house in Los Angeles."

"So you're never moving to Los Angeles?"

"No, I'll go visit Missy, but I live here. I'm hoping she will move here with me, that's why I bought this big house. I've lived in Tennessee since I was eighteen. I would go to California once in a while. When my brother died, Missy moved in with my mom. When my mom died, I told Missy the house was hers, but I would stay with her, or she could move to Tennessee with me."

Zane shook his head, "I don't think Missy wants to live alone. She was really scared when someone broke into her house. She stays with Rowan and Piper."

"I wanted her to move here with me, but she didn't want to. She said she didn't want to leave her friends. So why does she live with Rowan Scott and his wife?"

"Missy likes Piper. They are starting a charity for homeless families but enough serious talk for tonight. Why don't you get some sleep? I'll be up for the rest of the night."

"No, you don't have to stay up. I promise not to go outside again without waking you."

"Go to bed, Pollyanna. I'll be fine."

Reluctantly, Polly went to her room.

Zane couldn't get to sleep. He got up and made a cup of coffee. Then made himself an omelet. He thought about the guy who was hired to kill Pollyanna. Was he even looking for her? The guy already got his money. Did he take the money and decided that he would forget about killing Polly since Chester is dead. He got up and went to take a shower. He had just washed his hair when he heard the scream. He grabbed a towel and took off running. He ran into Polly's room. She was sitting up in bed. She looked like she saw a ghost.

"What happened?"

"I must have had a dream. I thought someone was in here. I'm sorry. Can you please check and see if anyone is in here?"

"Stay here." Zane tucked the towel more securely around his hips and went into the bathroom, then he looked inside the closet. He made sure the window was locked. Then he turned around and looked at her. "Lock this door. I'll check the rest of the house."

Polly jumped out of bed, "I'm going with you. She said as she ran to his side."

"Let me put some pants on."

Polly looked Zane over. "Damn, you're all muscles. What is this scar from? Look at this one. Are these bullet holes? How many do you have?" Polly touched his chest where a painful looking scar was. She let her hand linger a little longer than necessary.

"Move your hand, and don't look at me like that, or I'm going to take this towel off and that little thing you're wearing off of you."

Polly grabbed a large sweater from the foot of the bed and pulled it over her head. It fell to the bottom of her hips. She was wearing a worn out tank top and her panties, now she had the sweater on. She took his arm as they walked out of the room.

They walked into the next bedroom, where Polly turned her head while Zane pulled on some sweats. He picked up his gun and moved her behind him. They went from room to room. Everything was locked up tight. No windows had been opened, and the doors were locked. Zane checked the monitors on the cameras, and he didn't see anything.

He looked at Polly, "How would you like for me to make you some coffee and an omelet."

"Do you know how to cook?"

"Sure I do. I've been cooking for myself since I was seven."

"Seven-years-old. Why?"

"Because I was hungry. It was only eggs that I started

with, then I added toast. And then I would add other kinds of food. The lady next door would bring over food once in a while when my mom was gone." Zane didn't know why he told her about that time in his life so effortlessly. He's never told a soul about his life when he was young. It was something he wanted to forget.

"Where was your mom?"

"She was around sometimes, but she was usually passed out on the couch."

"I'm sorry but lucky for me, you can cook. I'm not much of a cook myself. I can cook a little. But I've never been interested in cooking. I've always been too busy writing songs and singing. It kind of took over my life."

"Even when you were little."

"Yeah, I'm actually shy around people. When I'm singing to them, I'm not shy. I've always had that problem. My parents thought that I had something wrong with me. I tried telling them I was just shy. They sent me to therapy."

"I would never have guessed you were shy."

"That's because I'm not shy with you. I feel comfortable with you."

Zane set her coffee and omelet in front of her. "I'm glad you feel like that with me. I feel comfortable with you too."

"This is delicious. Are you going to eat?"

"I had one earlier."

"What happened with your mom when you were little? Did she quit drinking?"

"No, my grandfather took me away from her when I was ten. I never saw her again. She drank herself to death, as far as I know. Who knows, she may still be alive, but I doubt it. My mom liked to party with alcohol and drugs."

Polly put her fork down, "I'm sorry."

"Yeah, me too. When my grandfather found me, he took me away, and I've never looked back. He had custody of me.

He let my mother visit with me when I was three-years-old, and she took me and disappeared. My grandfather looked for me for seven years before he found me. When I saw him at the door, I remembered him." Zane chuckled, "I threw my arms around him. I was almost as tall as he was. I didn't even turn around and get anything. My grandfather could see my mom passed out on the floor with one of her boyfriends, neither one of them had any clothes on. We left right then."

"Was your mother his daughter?"

"No, my dad died overseas. A mine blew up when he stepped on it. I was a baby. My grandfather had custody of me since I was six months old. He went to court when he found out his grandbaby lived on the streets."

"I'm glad he found you. How come it took him so long to find you?"

"He didn't have any money to hire someone to help him, plus he took care of my grandmother. She had a stroke and was bedridden. My mom took me to Mexico, where one of her boyfriends lived. They broke up, but we stayed there. My grandma died, and Grandpa was free to start hunting and asking people if they knew anything. Eventually, he found me."

"I'm glad he found you. Where is he now?"

"He died last year."

"I'm sorry."

"Yeah, I miss that old man. He was the most generous person I've ever known. He taught me everything. I never went to school until I went back home with him. We did home school until I caught up with my grade for a ten-year-old. My grandfather was a military man. He was a Green Beret, so when I graduated college, I joined the Navy Seals. I left after four years when my grandfather got cancer. He was upset until I became a DEA agent. Then I moved my grandfather and his nurse in with me. His nurse was a medic in the army, Warren. He's still living at my house even now. I like someone being there when I'm gone. Besides, I like Warren. He pretty much takes care of everything at home for me."

"So you're a softy."

"Don't let my kindness fool you. Most people I know don't want to speak to me. Believe me, there is nothing soft about me. "

Polly could believe that. She didn't see a soft spot on him. "Thanks for breakfast. I guess we better get ready to leave. A car is picking us up in an hour." She got off the stool and walked into her bedroom. She knew if she would have seen that naked chest another minute, she would have run her hands down his body and she wasn't too sure if she would stop things from going further.

3

Zane stood on stage while Pollyanna sang her songs. She looked over at him and smiled. The fans went wild. It was like this in every city they went to. When she turned and smiled at him, the ladies screamed.

"I have a new song to sing for you folks. I haven't recorded it yet. I just wrote it for my man. So you all will be the first to hear it. My band and I didn't have much time to practice, so if I mess up, ignore it, please." Polly laughed, then she started singing acapella until the band joined in.

Polly walked over to Zane and sang a love song to him. She leaned her body into his. Zane put his arms around her and kissed her neck. He kissed her bare shoulder. He nibbled her ear until she moaned into the microphone. Polly gazed into his eyes, and he could see the hot passion there. Pollyanna wanted him as much as he wanted her.

When the song finished, she whispered into his ear, "I wrote this song for you, Zane Taylor."

Zane kissed her lips. He knew tonight was the night. After six weeks together, they were going to stay in each other's arms tonight. Neither one of them could hold off another night.

POLLY COULDN'T WAIT to get back to the hotel. She wanted Zane. Polly craved him. He was all she could think of. Polly thought writing about him would help. Hell, she almost begged him to take her right there on stage. Tonight Zane Taylor would be hers. Polly wouldn't think about tomorrow. She would only think about tonight.

They didn't talk. Polly sat as close to Zane as possible on the ride to the hotel. Their rooms connected with a door between them. Zane didn't bother to go into his room. When the door closed, he stripped Polly of her top and discarded her bra with one snap. Zane cupped her breast with his hands before picking her up and laying her on the bed. He removed her jeans and put his hands at the edge of her panties.

"It's time for you to undress," Polly whispered. "I want to feel you against me. All of you."

Zane already had taken his shirt off; he stripped off the rest of his clothes. Polly watched him. He was magnificent. Zane crawled over to where she was and took off her underwear. Then he got on top of her and took a breast in his mouth. Polly moaned out loud. She thought she might have an orgasm before they made love. When he went down further, she knew for sure that she would.

Zane was having a hard time controlling himself; he wanted her more than anything. His body cried out for her. He was going to give her something first. He kissed his way down her body, his mouth touched her center, and his tongue made Pollyanna scream. She had an orgasm and then another before he entered her.

"Zane... Yes, it's perfect," she said, in a low whisper.

He looked into her eyes as she came, then he let his body release its built-up pressure. He collapsed on top of her. He kissed her neck and her breast, and he was ready to go again. He smiled. Polly wanted him too. They made love four times before falling asleep. She woke him up at five in the morning, wanting him. He loved making love with her. They didn't stop until the sun was high in the sky.

Zane pulled her closer to him. "What time do we leave?"

"I don't have to be in Los Angeles until tomorrow night. Why don't we stay in bed all day?"

"That's the best idea I've ever heard." He pulled her into him and closed his eyes, and both of them went to sleep.

Polly woke up and felt for Zane. She raised her head when she didn't touch him. She heard the shower. She smiled and threw her legs over the side of the bed. She could hear him singing as she pulled the curtain back and stepped in there with him.

Zane pulled her into his arms, he soaped her body all over while she did his. Polly reached down, he was so hard she wrapped her hand around him. She licked the side of Zane's neck. Then she licked her way down until she took him into her mouth. Zane moaned so loud he was surprised the person in the next room didn't hear him. He had a hold of Polly's head and pulled her up before he came.

"Fuck Pollyanna, are you trying to kill me. God, that was good." He kissed her long and hard as his fingers found her secret sensual spot. Polly came into his hand. They went back to bed and had hot passionate sex until the late afternoon when both of them became hungry.

Polly kissed him all over. She found a few more gunshot wounds she didn't see when she saw him with his shirt off. She traced them with her finger and kissed each one. He explained to her that they happened when he was a DEA agent. It took some convincing for her to believe that he wouldn't get shot anymore. He didn't need to tell her this job had its hazardous side as well.

"Let's order something from the restaurant here. That way, we won't have to leave the bed."

Zane nuzzled her neck, "I like the way your mind works."

Polly giggled, "Me too."

4

They landed in Los Angeles early. Ash picked them up and took them to Zane's house. Polly felt her face burning. She just knew that her face gave away that she and Zane have spent two days in bed having wild, passionate sex.

Ash looked at Aunt Polly, "You are nothing like we thought. Did Zane tell you we thought you were a senior citizen?"

Polly giggled and Zane chuckled. "Yeah, he told me."

"Pollyanna is nothing like I thought she was." Zane wanted to make sure the handsome Ash stayed away from what belongs to him. Ash had enough women chasing after him.

"Here I thought I would be in bed every night by eight, but Pollyanna keeps me awake until the early morning."

Polly elbowed him, "Zane means my concerts don't get over until late."

"Ash knew what I meant. Isn't that right, Ash?"

"Sure, I know exactly what Zane means."

"Do you know where Missy is? I would really love to see her while I'm in town," she attempted to change the topic.

"At the safe house. She's going to the concert tonight with all of us. She's excited to see you. If you want, we can stop at the safe house first."

"Is the safe house safer than your home?" Polly asked Zane.

"No."

Ash laughed, "No, home is safer than Zane's. When you step on his property without him knowing about it, the sirens go off. No one can get into his house. It locks down with a touch of a button."

"Why is it like that?"

"Because he was a top DEA agent. People wanted him dead. So he had to make sure he knew who was coming on his property."

"Thanks for scaring Pollyanna, Ash."

"He didn't scare me. I don't like it that people want you dead. I saw those scars." The moment that came out of her mouth, she felt her face burning.

"They don't want me dead any longer. I'm no longer a DEA agent. There is nothing to worry about. I promise you. Ash is talking out of his ass. Don't pay any attention to him."

"As long as you're safe, I won't worry. Besides, I'll be with you the entire time we're here."

Zane chuckled, *I better watch myself, or I'll find myself falling in love.* "Pollyanna, I hope you don't have any ideas in that pretty head of yours."

"Of course, I don't. I just remembered I'm in California, and I have a license to carry my gun."

"You are not carrying a gun. As soon as we get to my place, I want your gun. This isn't up for discussion."

Polly didn't say anything. There was no way she would hand over her gun to Zane. If he needed backup, then she would be ready. "I didn't bring my gun with me," she lied. "So you don't have to start ordering me around."

They were sitting in the backseat of Ash's vehicle, and he glanced in the rearview mirror at the same time Zane pulled Polly up next to him. Ash smiled. Zane was a man that women loved. Ash ignored the part about women loving him too. If Zane was with a woman for longer than two months, he let her know he wouldn't be getting serious. Zane wasn't going to fall in love with anyone ever, and marriage was out of the question. Zane has said that for the fifteen years Ash has known him.

When Ash pulled up to Zane's home, Polly's mouth fell open. There were trees in bloom everywhere. He pushed a button, and the gate opened. Polly got out of the car and laughed. It was the most beautiful landscaping she had ever seen. "My goodness, who did your landscaping? It's beautiful."

"Piper, she did all of it. Warren keeps it up for me. I was a little overwhelmed when I first saw all the flowers. She seems to enjoy pink a lot."

"I love it. What is that?" Polly walked over to the pond. There were fish swimming everywhere, the fish pond went under his house. "Where does it go?"

"Part of my floor is glass. You can see the fish swimming while inside."

"Are you kidding me? Damn, Piper is magnificent. I have never seen any landscaping this beautiful. Does she still take on jobs? Missy told me she's handed over a lot more of the work to her managers. I would love to have all of this in my yard in Tennessee."

"You'll have to talk to Piper. I'm sure she could do your yard. Let's walk around the back, and you can see what she did there."

Polly stopped and looked. It was all so amazing. The pool

looked like it went off the edge of the earth. Zane's backyard looked over the valley. Polly imagined when the sun went down it was stunning. "She's very talented."

"Yes, she is. You don't have to worry about Missy while she's with Piper and Rowan. Piper always has something going on. Remember I told you about their new charity? Missy will be busy for a few years with that. So you don't need to worry about her."

"I can't help it," she told the truth.

"She's in the safest place she could ever be. You'll see how happy she is when you see her. She loves what she's doing."

"Thank you, I was worrying, now I'm not. Missy has to have a project, or she gets bored fast."

"She has one now. Let's go inside."

"Where's Ash?"

"He had to get back to the house." They went in through the back door. The kitchen was a dream kitchen for a chef. A man was standing at the stove stirring something that smelled delicious. He turned around and smiled at them. Hey, I wondered when you were going to get here. Dinner will be ready in forty-five-minutes. He looked at Polly. "Sugar, I love your singing."

"Thank you. Please call me Polly. Dinner smells delicious. What is it?"

"Chili Verdi, I've been practicing my cooking on the guys at the safe house. They seem to like it."

"I'm sure it's delicious. I'm starving."

Warren smiled, and Polly saw his front tooth was gold. His hair was white and cut in the military-style. He wore cut-offs and no shoes. He was handsome, probably in his fifties. She realized she was staring and looked down. I'm sorry for staring. But you have the most beautiful eyes I have ever seen. What color are they?"

Zane laughed. "The first time I saw him, I asked him what

color his eyes were. He told me they change colors with what he's wearing. I thought he was lying to me. I used to watch him just to see if he had contacts. But they're his eyes. I call them sky-blue, violet, and gray. Am I right, Warren?"

"Yep, I used to get picked on because of them. That's why I learned to fight. My Dad taught me. So the bullies stopped making fun of me."

"Don't you think they were jealous of you? I mean, who wouldn't want your eyes? They are hot and sexy. Would you care if I wrote a song about your eyes?"

"Really, you want to write a song about my eyes?"

"Yes, I have it going around in my head right now—those sexy eyes."

"Sure, I can't wait to hear what you write."

"I'll sing it for you tomorrow if you want."

"Do I ever want?"

Zane knew what Warren wanted. "Let's put our bags away. Dinner will be ready when we finish." Pollyanna walked out of the kitchen, and Zane shook his fist at Warren, who held his hand over his heart. Zane chuckled as he shook his head. The minute they were alone, he pulled Polly into his arms and kissed her. Zane didn't think he would ever get enough of Pollyanna.

"Wow, this is your room?" Polly looked around. This was a man's bedroom with dark browns and olive greens. It was a nice room for a man. Polly liked whites. The bed dominated the room. It was the most enormous bed Polly had ever seen. When she walked into the bathroom, she stopped. Zane had a spa in his bathroom. She walked over to the Jacuzzi. It would easily hold four large people. The shower had three rain heads on the ceiling and on the walls. No matter where you stood taking a shower, you would get sprayed by all the spouts. Polly looked over at Zane. "How many people have been in this shower at one time?"

"You're the only person who has been in my room. So we'll try it out after dinner."

"Your home is magnificent. Are you sure you want me here?"

"Why would you ask that?"

"Well, you said no one has been here. So if you want, I can stay at the safe house with the others?"

"No." Zane took a step closer and put his arms around her. "I want you with me. I want you with me here. I've never wanted to bring anyone else here. That's why no one has been here before." He kissed her neck, and before she realized what he was doing, her top was off, and he pushed her over to the bed. It only took them a minute to get their other clothes off. They made love for thirty-five minutes. It was hot and crazy. Let's go eat, then we'll come back and take a shower before your concert."

"No, I'll take a shower by myself, or I'll be late for my concert."

Zane laughed. He put his arm around Pollyanna and kissed her as they walked to the kitchen.

ZANE WATCHED his friends in the audience singing and dancing. Polly sang with a male country singer. The song had the audience dancing. He looked over at Polly and Luke singing. Zane thought Luke was dancing too close to Pollyanna. One thing Zane knew how to do was dance. He walked up to his sweetheart and took her in his arms. If someone was going to dance sexy with Polly, then it was going to be him.

Polly threw her arms around him when he walked up to her and took her in his arms. Damn, he could dance. Polly took dancing lessons for ten years. She loved dancing sexy. By the time the song was over, Polly was ready to leave and crawl into bed with this handsome man she thought she might be falling in love with. No, she had fallen in love.

Zane pulled her close and kissed her thoroughly, "I can't wait until I have you in my bed. And don't forget you promised to shower with me," he whispered in her ear while he kissed her again. When he looked at Polly, her eyes told him she would leave right now if she could. He let her go and walked to the back of the stage. When he looked at his friends, they were going crazy. Missy was clapping and cheering them on to dance some more.

5

Zane opened his eyes and looked for Polly. *What time is it?* He looked at his phone. It was already nine. He threw the covers back and jumped in the shower. He heard Pollyanna singing to Warren. How the hell was she able to write a song so fast? He walked into the kitchen. Polly sat on a stool with her guitar singing while Warren cooked breakfast. After last night staying up most of the night making love, he was surprised to see Polly looking so bright-eyed. She was beautiful. Zane felt something he's never felt before. Something he didn't want. He didn't want to feel these different feelings for Polly. But here they were. He would have to try and distance himself from her. When the song ended, he clapped as loud as Warren did.

"You have another hit, Polly," Zane said, clapping.

Polly bowed to both men, while her mind was thinking that Zane has never called her Polly. He has always called her Pollyanna. "Thank you."

"I love this song. I'm honored my eyes gave you the inspiration to write this beautiful song."

As soon as breakfast was finished, they left. Polly wanted

to ask Zane if something was wrong, but he looked like he was deep in his own thoughts. Just because they enjoyed each other didn't mean there was more to it. Polly knew she should remember that. "Do you like living in California?" *Why the hell did I ask him that? He'll think I want him to move to Tennessee.* "Yeah, I like California. I get pissed at the politicians, but that's life. Nothing is ever perfect."

"How about you? Do you like living in Tennessee?"

"I told you I do. But I moved to Tennessee mostly for my career. Now that I have made a name for myself, I can move anywhere."

"What time is your concert tonight?"

"I need to be there by six. Is something wrong?"

Zane didn't want to hurt her, but he had to make her understand nothing could come of this. He has always promised himself and his grandfather he would never fall in love. He wished they could keep on seeing each other, but he didn't want her falling in love with him either. He never stayed with a woman long enough to fall in love. Yet, he didn't want to be away from her even for a minute. He knew when he saw her dancing with her singing partner Luke last night, he was jealous. Jealousy implies you had feelings for that person. He needed to stop this now. Falling in love means someone was going to get hurt. He didn't want to hurt Pollyanna. So it was better if he broke it off right now before she started loving him.

When he pulled into the driveway of the safe house, he turned and looked at her. "I want to be with you, Polly. But I'm not going to allow myself to fall in love with you. That would only bring pain for you. I think before you fall in love with me, we should take a step back from each other. We've had a great time together, and we could still have a good time, but I don't want to hurt you."

"Are you telling me this because I leave my things lying around?"

"No, I don't care about how messy you are."

"I wouldn't call myself messy. I mean, I've never seen anyone as neat as you. But I don't understand why you think I would fall in love with you. I thought we were having a good time. Maybe I got the wrong idea. I thought you enjoyed being with me."

"I do. I love being with you. I don't want a serious relationship."

"If you want us to take a step back, then that's what we will do. Our staying up most of the night having sex is wearing me out anyway. Besides, if sex is what I want, Luke is always there." *Polly, don't you dare cry in front of Zane. If he wants us to stay away from each other, then I will stay away from him.*

Zane was becoming angry. What the hell did she mean Luke was there. "What the hell do you mean Luke is there?"

"I don't mean anything. Why would you think I would fall in love with you?"

"I don't want to hurt you. I care for you. I don't want you to think it could go any further than it is."

"Wow, Zane, do you think because I enjoy having sex with you, I'm going to break down and profess how much I love you?" It took all Polly had to laugh. She didn't know if she pulled it off or not. She opened the car door and climbed out. Missy came out of the house and threw her arms around her.

"You have to teach me how to dance."

"Yeah, right. I've seen you dance. I missed you, sweetheart."

"I miss you too. How long do you get to stay?"

"I have to leave tomorrow. I'll be back sometime after my

tour is over. That's in two months. Tell me about this charity of yours and Piper's?"

"It's for homeless families. Not all homeless people are drug attacks or alcoholics. Some families live on the streets and in their cars because they can't afford to rent a home. I have met so many homeless families since we've started this charity drive. It's so sad to meet these families with small children living on the street. Can you imagine how the parents must feel? A lot of the time, it's only the mother and kids. I'm determined to help them."

"I'm so proud of you. I always knew you would find something like this. You have a heart of gold. When do you go back to school?"

Missy laughed. "In October, I'll go three days a week and see if they can teach me something I don't know."

"I want to donate to your charity. Give me the information before I leave."

"Okay, I will. So tell me about you and Zane?"

"What's to tell? We enjoyed each other, but now Zane's afraid I'm going to fall in love with him. Can you imagine that?" Polly shook her head. "Me falling in love."

Missy looked into her Aunt Polly's eyes, "Oh my God, you love him."

"Shhhh, why would you say that?" Polly whispered, looking around to see where Zane was.

"I can see it in your eyes."

"Damn it. Do you think Zane could see? Of course, he could. That's why he wants to take a step back. I'm an idiot."

"You are not. What did he say to you?"

"He wants us to take a step back before I fall in love with him."

"I think he wants to take a step back because he's falling in love with you."

"I don't think so. Zane always seems to have control of everything."

"He didn't have control when you were dancing with Luke last night. It took him less than a minute to walk over and put you in his arms instead of Luke's. I saw the way he looked at you."

"It doesn't matter. I'm going to tell Ash I want a different bodyguard. I no longer want to be with someone afraid of falling in love with me. Screw him. I'll have a new bodyguard."

"Oh, yeah. That should make Zane angry, and we'll see if he gets jealous."

"Missy, I don't want Zane to be jealous. It's different with us. If he wants this thing between us to stop, then it's going to stop right now. I don't want to have him as my bodyguard. I don't know why I let my guard down with him, but it won't happen again. Let's go inside."

Polly said hello to everyone. Zane was looking at her differently; she thought he couldn't figure out if he wanted to keep her or not. She decided to make a choice herself. Polly saw Ash walk into the kitchen and followed him.

"Ash, I want to talk to you about my bodyguard."

"What's up with Zane?"

"I don't want him to be my bodyguard anymore. If you don't have anyone available, I'll go to another company."

"I thought you and Zane were doing great together."

"We were, but he decided he was afraid I was falling in love with him. I don't want him worrying about me falling for him. Do you have anyone else?"

"Yeah, Rhys can guard you starting tonight."

"Great, can you please have someone get my belongings from Zane's house?"

"Yeah, I will take care of everything. When do you leave?"

"Tonight after the concert. I already bought the tickets to

Hawaii. I have a concert there tomorrow night, then I have one on Saturday night in New York. After my tour, I won't need your services any longer. I'm going to disappear for a while. No one will know where I am. I've also hired someone who will hunt the man down. I've been on my own since I was eighteen. I'm not going to allow another person to tell me what I can and cannot do. If that man gets close to me, I'll shoot his sorry ass," she said sternly before pausing. "Okay, I think that's all I need. If you can have someone bring my things to my hotel that would be great. I'm leaving now, my taxi is outside. Here's the name of my hotel. You can give it to Rhys."

"Wait, Rhys will go with you. If the killer is anywhere, he's here in Los Angeles."

"I told Missy goodbye. I'll be outside waiting."

∼

FUCK, what the hell did Zane tell her? Ash walked out back and told Rhys he would be guarding Polly if he needed to grab his bag to do it now. They always kept their bag full of everything they would need if they had to hurry off like now. He waited for them to leave before talking to Zane.

"Zane, can I talk to you?"

"What's up?"

"You'll no longer be Polly's bodyguard."

"What the fuck are you talking about?"

"Rhys has taken over for you. She no longer wants you as her bodyguard."

"Did she say why?"

"Yes, she said you were worried she was falling in love with you. So I guess she decided you didn't need to worry about that anymore."

"Where is she?"

"She's gone. Rhys is with her, so you don't have to worry about her falling in love with you. I have another case for you starting tonight. Here's the file. Can you get Polly's things from your house? I'll drop them off at her hotel."

"I'll drop them off myself. What hotel is she staying at?"

"You're off the case. That means you will not contact Polly. I don't know what the fuck you said to her, but she's pissed off. Stay away from her. She has a concert tonight, so she needs her mind free of stress."

Zane took it hard hearing this but his friend was right and Polly was right for doing what she felt necessary. "You can follow me home, and I'll get her things."

"Let me get my keys."

∼

ZANE WALKED up the stairs to his room, wondering if he screwed up something extraordinary. He chuckled when he saw Pollyanna's things on the floor of his bathroom. He remembered taking that top off of her early this morning. He decided not to give it back to her. He hurried and packed all of her belongings in her suitcase. He carried it to Ash. *Did I screw up?* He handed Ash her belongings.

"What the fuck did you do? Hell, you were the one falling in love. That's it, isn't it? You had to scare her off before she found out you were in love with her."

"You don't know what the fuck you're talking about."

"Don't I? You haven't changed since college. I bet this is the first time it backfired on you."

"I don't have time to talk to you. I have to get to my next case."

Ash laughed as he drove away. He didn't have the time to figure out Zane's love life. He couldn't even take care of his, well, in his case, lack of a love life.

~

Rhys sat at the back of the stage and watched Polly's rehearsal. He wondered what happened with her and Zane. Then his thoughts went to Julia. She was going to kill herself if she wasn't careful. She was working with some bad dudes, and she acted like she has nine lives. He didn't have the time to worry about Julia right now. He would call Skye Ryan and see if she knows what is going on with her when he got the chance.

Polly turned around and smiled at Rhys with his stormy gray eyes and his jet black hair. He was a handsome man. Why don't we order in for dinner? What do you like to eat?"

Rhys chuckled, "I like just about everything."

"We'll order Chinese food."

"That sounds good to me. I have to warn you, though, I don't know how to dance."

Polly laughed, "I'm pretty sure Zane is the only one I want to dance with."

"Then why did you change bodyguards?"

"He thought to tell me not to fall in love with him. What a dumb ass. I'm pretty sure if I saw him again, I would slug him."

Rhys shook his head, "Yeah, he is a stupid ass."

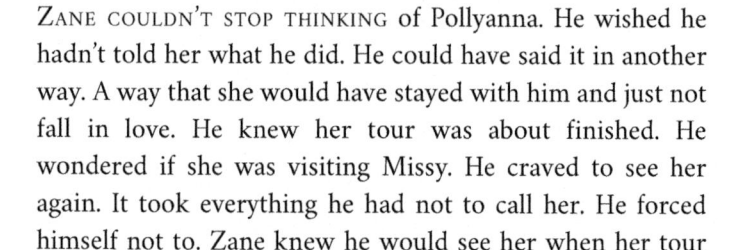

~

Zane couldn't stop thinking of Pollyanna. He wished he hadn't told her what he did. He could have said it in another way. A way that she would have stayed with him and just not fall in love. He knew her tour was about finished. He wondered if she was visiting Missy. He craved to see her again. It took everything he had not to call her. He forced himself not to. Zane knew he would see her when her tour was over. Rhys would bring her to the safe house. They were all meeting there tonight. Maybe she was already there. He all of a sudden looked forward to something. He hadn't been excited about anything since he chased Pollyanna away.

Zane spotted Rhys as soon as he walked in the front door. He looked around and didn't see Pollyanna. "Where's Pollyanna?"

Rhys looked at the dumb ass, "I don't know. I haven't seen her since she decided she doesn't need a bodyguard."

"What the fuck are you talking about?"

"Polly said she was fine. She was going to disappear for a while. She promised me if she feels like she's being stalked, she would get a hold of us."

"And you just let her go on her own?"

"What did you want me to do?"

"You could have told her no. What happens if that guy finds her? Fuck. Tell me where she is, and I'll go to her."

"I don't know where she is. I told you she said she was going to disappear. She's not telling anyone where she is."

Zane hunted Ash down, "Do you know where Pollyanna is?"

"No, I haven't spoken to her since you told her not to fall in love with you."

"Don't be a smart ass, Ash. Did you know she doesn't have a bodyguard?"

"I knew she wasn't going to have us after her tour ended. I'm surprised she didn't find someone else. Is that what Rhys said?"

"Yes, he said she didn't want a bodyguard. That guy who was hired to kill her is still out there."

"Maybe he decided to keep the money and not kill her."

"And maybe he didn't. I'm going to find Pollyanna. Is Arrow here?"

"Yes, he's here."

Zane didn't hear him. He already walked away.

Zane explained to Arrow why he wanted his wife Brinley to find Polly. That's when Ash walked up and shook his head.

"No."

"What do you mean no?"

Ash frowned at Zane. "I mean, Polly doesn't want us to find her. She's taking a break from touring. You should respect that. She told me when Rhys took over that she would be going where no one could find her. Look, Zane, you did this. Polly didn't. How could she stay with you after you told her what you did? You never knew anything about how to talk to women. Women get their feelings hurt easily. Especially if she was falling in love with you. Which I doubt she was. You would be a hard man to love. I mean, look at how you always go around straightening things up. You can be here thirty minutes, and everything is picked up."

Rhys laughed, "Yeah, and how you never have a wrinkle in your clothes. You redo the paperwork you're given if it has wrinkles. You are so used to being the boss sometimes you start bossing people around who are near you."

"I don't want to hear anymore. If you two find this funny, then there is something wrong with you." He turned to look at Arrow, "What do you think?"

"I think if she wants you to find her, she will call and tell you where she is. Brinley would feel the same as I do."

Zane wanted to punch someone. "When is this damn meeting going to take place?"

"Right now," Ash said, walking into the main room where all the Seals were. "Listen, up everyone." The room went quiet and everyone gave him their full attention. "We are going to be taking over a high-security job. You will have to carry your weapons with you all the time. There will be four men at a time, then you will be relieved after two weeks. Another four men will take over. This job is going to be strenuous on everyone involved. That's why we will relieve each other every two weeks. We will be taking care of a mother and her baby. An ex-father-in-law wants her dead. Her husband was murdered when he decided to leave the mob. Now the father-in-law wants the child. The problem is there is no proof that it is him. They have tried everything to take the baby and kill the mother. I haven't met her. I've talked to her father, who hired us. He said she has so far escaped death, but it gets worse each time. He said no matter where she runs to, he finds her. He's afraid this next time, the father-in-law will kill her. So we have her in Alaska at our safe house there. Storm and Jonah are with her right now. Rhys and Zane can join Storm and Jonah. Then Marc, Kane, Austin, and I will relieve you. We'll use the company jet. That way, we won't be tracked. Does anyone have any questions?"

"What about Polly? I have to find her and make sure she's safe."

Ash looked like he was ready to slam his fist into Zane's face. "You have one month. If you haven't found Polly by that time, you're on your own. You no longer work for us."

Zane nodded his head once. He turned around and left the room.

"I'll call Killian. He'll be on the first shift with you, Rhys."

"Okay, I'll head out to the airstrip."

6

Brinley wouldn't help him find where Pollyanna had taken off to. She told him if Polly wanted to be alone, he should respect her wishes. Zane called Shay to see if she knew where Pollyanna was. She hadn't seen her either, at least that's what she said. He contacted Luke, he said he didn't know where she went, but he knew she wanted to be alone. He told Zane he should stop trying to find her.

Zane was disgusted with himself for telling Pollyanna they needed to take a step back. He didn't want to take a step back. He loved her. Zane wanted to be with her forever. He admitted to himself that it was he who was getting too close. Zane remembered his grandfather telling him almost every day not to fall in love. He would say it will destroy you. That's what happened to Zane's father, he would say. He had fallen so in love with Zane's mother it killed him when she became hooked on drugs and left him. She never told him about the baby she was pregnant with. Zane's father died in Iran not long after Zane was born. When his mother showed up at the funeral with her baby and drug-addicted friends, his grandfather went to court and got full custody of Zane.

And now here he was doing the one thing his grandfather told him not to do. He had fallen in love, even though he tried not to. Zane had to tell Pollyanna he loved her. But first, he had to find her.

～

POLLY HAD no idea that Zane tried to find her. In fact, she would have been pissed if she knew. Polly still couldn't get over him, telling her they needed to take a step back. That hurt. She had already fallen in love with Zane. Polly thought he felt the same way she did. He held her as if he loved her. Zane kissed her as if he loved her. He made love to her as if he loved her. Polly thought about it over and over these last few months. She knew Zane loved her, but it was up to him to come to that realization. She decided it was time to come out of hiding. She called Missy and told her she was going home to Tennessee. "Hi Missy, I miss you, sweetie."

"Where are you?"

"I'm heading home now. I don't have anything scheduled. I'm taking some time off. Come and see me whenever you have time."

"I will. I miss you too. I'll call you tonight and fill you in on what is going on with me."

"Okay, I'll talk to you later, bye honey."

Polly was home for two weeks when Zane showed up. She almost fell on her ass when she opened the door, and he stood there looking as handsome as ever.

He had his duffle bag slung over his shoulder and waited for her to ask him in. As soon as the door closed behind him, he dropped his duffel bag and stepped closer to Polly. He watched for a reaction from her. His heart was thundering away in his chest. It was so loud he thought for sure Polly could hear it. He didn't know where to start. He decided to start from the beginning.

"Can I talk to you?"

"Let's go sit down. What is it, Zane? Please hurry and tell me. I don't know how long I can sit here without crying."

"I was wrong. It wasn't you who was falling in love. It was me. I was worried about falling in love. While I lived with my grandfather, he told me every day to never let myself fall in love. He said it would ruin me like it ruined my father. I fell in love with you the first time I stood on stage with you. It scared the hell out of me. I told myself I was wrong; I wouldn't fall in love. I wasn't my father, and you damn sure weren't my mother. If you only knew the anguish I went through falling in love with you. After you fired me from your case, I didn't know what to do. I love you so much, but I didn't want you to know. I was afraid. Then I knew I had to stop acting like a fool and tell you how I felt. But I couldn't find you. Can you ever forgive me?"

Polly stood up and walked to the window. She watched a mother bird feeding her babies. It's been three months since she last saw Zane. Three months of not hearing anything from him. She put her hand on her tummy, thinking about her baby. She didn't want to tell Zane about the baby. If he didn't want her for herself, then she didn't want him either. Who was she fooling? She wanted Zane. Polly loved him; her heart was broken because of the way he brushed her off. Did he even know he broke her heart?

"Zane, you broke my heart. I'm sorry your grandfather poisoned your mind against falling in love. I can't let myself be hurt by you again. If you let what your grandfather said to you when you were growing up come between us, then what else will you allow to come between us? What else did he say about falling in love? Did he tell you it was alright to hurt someone without a thought to how that person would feel?"

"No, I'm not blaming my grandfather. I'm the one who hurt you. Sure, my grandfather may have warped my mind. But he's gone. I messed up on my own. Hell, I'm thirty-six. I think that makes me old enough to speak for myself. I never came close to falling in love until I met you. That scared the hell out of me. These new feelings scared the hell out of me."

"Do these feelings scare you enough that you'll want to take a step back three months from now? I can't be with you if you aren't sure if you love me. Or if you let your memories of your grandfather telling you how horrible it is if you allow yourself to fall in love."

"No, sweetheart, I promise I'll never want to take a step back from you ever again. I love you. I have never said that to another person."

"Do you think if you had allowed yourself to fall in love with someone else, you would have loved her as much as you love me?"

Zane smiled and walked closer to Polly, "No, I would never have fallen in love with anyone else. I have only ever loved you."

Polly wiped tears from her eyes and smiled, "I love you too."

Zane gathered her up in his arms. He would never let anything come between them again. "I'm sorry, darling, I'll never hurt you again, I promise you. I became so scared when I couldn't find you."

"I went away for a while. I had to think about some things."

"About me?"

"Among other things. I'm going to take some time off of touring for a year or two. Are you on an assignment right now?"

Zane kissed her, "Yes. I missed you so much. I have a couple days, then I have to leave."

"I'm glad you can stay. I missed you too." Polly decided not to mention the baby. She wanted to wait and tell him after knowing he wanted her for herself and not the baby. "Would you like something to drink? I'm actually cooking dinner tonight. I've been working on some new meals. Healthy meals."

"That sounds great. Where did you go to get away?"

"I stayed at a friend's place while she was in Europe. Oh, by the way, Missy's going to come for a couple of weeks before school starts."

"That should be fun. Missy's a great kid."

"She is, isn't she? Thank you, I'm so proud of her."

Zane walked into Polly's room with his bag. He looked around and smiled. He bent down and picked up her nightshirt. He folded it up and set it on the chair in the corner.

"Where is your assignment?"

"Alaska, we're doing two weeks on and two weeks off."

"Can you talk about it?"

"We are guarding a woman and her baby who is in hiding from her father-in-law. Who

has ties to the mob? He's trying to take the child away from her and to kill her in the process."

"Please be careful when you go there. We still have two nights."

"Yes, we do. What are you cooking?"

"Grilled fish and a Mediterranean salad. I also have some sweet tea."

"You must have known I was coming. You're cooking my favorite dish."

They had the best two nights they ever had. Zane didn't want to leave. He told Polly a hundred times he loved her. He poured all the love he felt for her into their lovemaking. He didn't need words to tell her how much he loved her. Zane showered her with love.

"I wish you didn't have to go, but I know you do. Please be careful."

"I will. I'll see you in a few weeks. I love you, darling. I want you to be careful as well. I'll call you when I can. Zane pulled her into his arms and kissed her as if he wouldn't see her in a long time.

"I love you too, Zane. I always will."

7

"Well, look who's here. Did you find Polly?" Rhys asked, grinning.

"Yes, I found her. I poured my heart out to her, and she forgave me for being a stupid ass."

"Good, now you can get to work, and I can get back home to my family," Killian said, slapping him on the back.

"Yes, I heard the baby will be here any day. I talked to Brinley. She's been staying with Bird in case she goes into labor. Killian, thanks for covering for me."

"Hey, I'm in love. I know how it feels when something isn't going right. I'll introduce you to Willow and the baby."

Zane followed Killian into the kitchen. Willow turned from feeding the baby.

"Willow, this is Zane Taylor. He'll be taking my place while I get back to my wife."

"Hello Willow, what is this little sweetie's name?" Zane asked while watching the baby girl eating. She had more food on her than in her mouth, and she thought it was funny. The more she laughed, the more food got on her face in her nose. She even had food in her hair. Her hands and arms were covered in baby food. Zane backed up so he didn't get food on his clothes.

"Her name should be messy, but it's Ruby. Be careful; nothing makes her laugh harder than when her food lands on someone's clothes." Willow looked at Zane's clothes, and she knew they were expensive.

"Hi, Ruby, you don't want to throw your food on me now, do you, sweet baby girl?" Zane laughed as Ruby smiled at him. Look at that tooth. You are so cute," Zane bent closer to the baby, and he got a handful of food thrown on his shirt. He stood up straight and looked at his shirt. "Who eats orange food? I wonder if it comes out in the wash."

"Ruby, that's not nice. Look what you did to Zane's shirt. I'm so sorry, I can never get it out of my clothes. Maybe if you soak it right now, it'll come out."

"Don't worry about it. Ruby was just having fun, weren't you, baby."

Killian laughed. "Bye, I have a plane to catch."

"See you around Killian, let us know when the baby comes."

"Do you mind holding Ruby since you already have food on you? I need to start her some bathwater," She handed the baby to a stuned Zane.

Zane watched as Willow walked out of the kitchen. He looked at the baby and held her out away from him. Hell, he didn't know what to do with a baby. He did know she was covered from head to toe with orange baby food. "I'm taking your clothes off of you," Zane said as he sit the baby on the table and stripped her clothes off of her. "I don't want any more orange food on me. What is this crap anyway? I think while I'm with you I'll make you something to eat. They must put food coloring in baby food. That can't taste good. There," he said, "now, do you feel better having those dirty clothes off." Zane smiled at Ruby, who hadn't taken her eyes off of him. "Here, let me put this towel around you." He grabbed a kitchen towel and put it around her.

"Oh, you've already taken her clothes off for me. Thank you."

"She was trying her best to put more food on me. I figured the best thing to do is to take them off of her. I hope you didn't mind."

"No, I'm happy to get help when I can. I'm so thankful my father found you guys before Geno managed to kill me. He's not going to give up. I know him."

"We won't let any harm come to you or Ruby. Don't worry, we'll take care of everything."

Willow nodded and left to give her baby a bath.

Zane changed his shirt and soaked it in the sink before he went to talk to the others. They were in the room with all the cameras. He shut the door, so they couldn't be overheard. It still amazed him that Piper's parents did all of this so the Russians wouldn't find them. They were Russian spies who always thought they were Americans until they turned eighteen. That's when the Russians contacted them and told them what they were supposed to do. They hid from the Russians until they died in a boat accident.

"What do we know about Geno Russo?"

"He's a crazy son of a bitch. He won't stop until he kills Willow and takes Ruby."

"That won't be happening. So it's either Willow's life or his."

Rhys looked at Zane and shook his head. "Zane, I know you're used to killing anyone who needs killing, but we don't go around killing people. We have to get proof he's out to kill Willow, then he will be locked up."

Zane laughed, "Are you fucking kidding me. They won't lock this guy up. His type buys his way out of everything. The men he hires to kill for him always end up dead. So don't think he'll be sent to prison. The guy won't even spend one night in jail." Zane had been a DEA agent for years, so he knows how these men get away with everything including murder.

Rhys looked at the others, "Have either of you come up with something?"

"Ash is looking into this guy's past. He has someone helping him with it too. It might be Brinley, I'm not sure, but he'll get in touch with us when he knows something. In the meantime, we guard Willow and Ruby and make sure the bastard doesn't find them."

Zane looked at the men, "I'll take the first shift tonight so you guys can get some sleep whenever you want to."

Ash turned to look at Zane, "I'm glad you found Polly and worked it all out. Always remember women have gentle feelings." He held his hand up when Zane started to say something, "I know what you're going to say. Even though our female FBI friends can kick ass, they still have gentle feelings. If you don't believe me, ask their husbands."

"I'm starting to figure out all of this. But thanks for the advice."

"That's me, Mr. Advice giver. I've never fallen in love, but I have three sisters, two of whom are detectives for the Los Angeles police department. So I know how women's minds work."

"Yeah, I seem to remember when one of those two arrested the district attorney of Los Angeles for molestation charges. If I remember correctly, he's still in prison."

"He died in prison. Prisoners don't like child molesters."

"Go get some sleep. I'm going to call Pollyanna."

Zane waited for Polly to answer the phone. He almost hung up, thinking she was sleeping when it was picked up. "Hey sweetheart, did I wake you up?"

"No, I was in the shower. How is everything going there?"

"Everything is fine here. I met a six-month-old little person. She threw food all over my shirt. Zane laughed, "Her name is Ruby, and she's adorable. What have you been doing, love?"

"Well, since it was this morning I last saw you, I haven't done much. Tell me about the baby?"

"There isn't much to tell. When I saw her, there was orange food all over her. I'll never get it out of my shirt. They must put food coloring in the baby food to make it so bright."

"I'm sure they do. They put it in everything else." Polly smiled to herself. "I'm painting one of my bedrooms." She wouldn't tell him about the baby until she was sure he loved her.

"Oh, yeah. What color?"

"It's a beautiful light yellow. I used to do all the painting when I stayed at my mom's house. She didn't trust anyone to come into her home. Oh Zane, I already miss you."

"I miss you too, sweetheart. I wanted to call and tell you goodnight."

"Goodnight, Zane, stay safe."

∼

POLLY WASN'T KIDDING when she said she missed Zane. He's all she ever thinks about anymore. She put her pajamas on and crawled in bed. Then she decided to check all the doors to make sure they were locked. As she walked around the house, she couldn't help but think of her baby. She wondered if Zane would be angry with her for waiting to tell him he would be a father in about six months. Polly shrugged her shoulders. He will have to get over it.

Her phone rang again as she crawled into bed. She smiled as she picked it up. "Don't tell me you wanted to tell me how much you love me again." There was no answer. "Hello."

"Zane, are you there." *They must be having bad weather or something.* Polly laid the phone down and cuddled the pillow Zane used. It still smells as good as he does. Before she knew it, she was sleeping. The phone ringing woke her up in the wee hours of the morning.

Polly reached for it, still half asleep. "Hello."

"Humm, I wonder who that was." She glanced at the time. It was almost four. *I'll sleep for another hour or two.*

"When her phone woke her up again, she wasn't happy. She grabbed it, "Hello."

"Hi Aunt Polly, did I wake you up. It's nine o'clock."

"Missy, I'm sorry for being grumpy. My phone woke me up twice last night. Someone must have been trying to call someone and had the wrong number."

"Sorry about that. Let's hope they found the right person and won't call you anymore. Anyway, I thought I would come for a visit before school starts like I promised."

"Oh, Missy, I've been looking forward to that. I can't wait to see you. Let me know when your plane gets in, and I'll meet you there."

Polly was so happy, she didn't realize how much she missed her niece until she heard her voice. *There is so much to do, I need to go to do some shopping before Missy gets here. I need to wash her bedding. It's been a while since anyone has slept in that room.*

She almost called Zane and share her news but decided not to bother him. *I think I'll go shopping first.* She put on her cap she wore in case someone spotted her in Target. Polly backed out of the garage and drove down her driveway to her gate, which she noticed was open. *I know I closed those gates. Maybe I thought I did. No one can open the gate without the remote, and I have both of them. I'm sure I'm worrying about nothing.* Polly decided to stop thinking about it. She convinced herself that she forgot to close the gates after Zane left yesterday. *I have to be more careful. When I get home, I'll check the cameras.*

She walked through the grocery store, picking up all foods Missy liked. Then she decided she would buy some good movies for them to watch. She wasn't going to tell Missy about the baby either, that would be her secret, for now.

8

"Missy, I'm so glad you could visit. Though, I must confess, I wish you could stay longer."

"Me too. I have missed you so much. But school starts next week, or I would stay another two weeks." They put Missy's suitcases in the trunk and drove down the driveway. "Your gate is open."

"I'm having trouble with it. I had the guy come out and look at it. He said there was nothing wrong with it, but it keeps opening by itself."

"You should have another company put a new gate up. The people you have apparently don't care if it works or not. Get another company. In fact, I'm going to make you an appointment for this afternoon."

"Oh Missy, there you go," she chuckled.

"What? We have to be careful, especially because you refuse to have a bodyguard."

Polly looked across at Missy lovingly. "I miss you taking control of everything. It has been great having that these past few days. It gets a bit lonely here all on my own."

"It keeps slipping my mind to ask you. What happened to Jennifer your assistant? I thought you liked her."

"I do like her. She moved to Alabama."

"You should find someone else."

"I will, but I'm taking some time off, so I'll wait until I'm back on the road working. I want you to take care of yourself, Missy. I'm glad you're working with Piper. You are doing something good. I'm so proud of you. Your grandma is smiling down from heaven. Sometimes I wish I had a regular job. I'm burned out right now. Once I have some time off, I'll be ready to go back to work. Call me when you get home, sweetie."

"I will," Missy said as she got her suitcase from the trunk of the car.

∼

"Hi, sweetheart."

"Zane, are you coming to visit me?"

"Yes, I'll be there tomorrow morning. How was your visit with Missy?"

"It was wonderful. Missy is such a good person. She has a heart of gold. I am so proud of the woman she has become. I can't wait to see you, Zane. What time does your plane get in? I'll pick you up?"

"I'll call you when I find out. I love you, Pollyanna. More than I can say. I can't wait to see you."

"I love you to Zane. I'll see you tomorrow."

∼

"Zane look at this? Are those footprints in the snow?"

"Fuck, did someone go outside?"

"None of us."

"Get Willow and Ruby. Take them into the tower room. They found us. How the hell did they find us?"

Willow ran into the room with Ruby. "I saw someone looking into the window. What's going on?"

"Go to the tower room with Rhys. Hurry, go!"

Rhys grabbed the bag they kept packed for the baby. He put Willow in front of him, and they ran upstairs. Once in there, they pushed a button, and the room locked down. No one could get inside. The windows were shattered proof.

"How did he find us?" Willow cried. "I thought we were safe."

"Did you call anyone?"

"What? Only my mom. She's the only one I called. I knew she would be worried."

"You might as well have called your ex-father-in-law and told him where you were." He watched out the window as Zane went around the back of the house. Storm ran around the other side. Rhys pushed a button on his vest. "Storm, there is a man behind the second tree on your left."

"Gotcha," he heard a whispered voice. Rhys watched as Storm stopped and turned. His gun was aimed when the man jumped away from the tree. One-shot, and the man was dead.

Rhys turned to Willow, "See if you can see anyone from the other window. Tell me what you see, and I can let the guys know."

Willow ran across the room after putting Ruby in the playpen they put in there earlier. Willow couldn't see anything, then she spotted Zane, walking backward toward the house, as she watched a man stepped out from the deck and aimed his gun. "Zane!" she screamed.

Rhys did the same thing when he shouted Zane's name. Zane swung around and fired his gun. The man fired his weapon at the same time. Both of them fell down. Willow cried out,

"Zane's been shot."

"Is he moving?"

Willow watched Zane, "Yes, he's up and holding his shoulder."

"Keep looking. I wish we knew how many there were out there. That way, we would know how many more there are." He looked closely at the trees, "Storm, to your right. I see movement. Wait, it's Jonah. He has blood coming from his side. It looks like he's hurt. Zane is walking toward you. He's been shot in the shoulder. Fuck, Jonah went down. We need to get out of here before more come. I don't see anymore." He turned and looked at Willow. "Do you see any movement anywhere, Willow?"

"No, I don't see anyone. Where will we go? I brought on all of this when I called my mother."

"That's why we said not to call anyone. We have other places to go. Don't worry. We won't let anything happen to you or Ruby."

"I don't want anyone dying, except my damn father-in-law. I should have hired someone to kill him."

"Don't say stuff like that. You never know whose listening."

"Rhys, we're leaving. Get Willow and the baby down here." Storm said into the speaker. "You'll have to take her and the baby on the plane to Zane's house. It's the safest place right now. Do you remember how to fly?"

"Yes." Rhys checked Zane and Jonah's wounds.

"Rhys, can you call Pollyanna and tell her I won't see her until we get Willow taken care of. Don't tell her I've been shot."

"Don't you think you should call her? Polly will know something is wrong if I call."

"You're right. I didn't want to have to lie to her, but I'll handle it. You need to leave, we're going to follow you to the airport. Then we'll go to the hospital. We need to get out of here before anyone else shows up."

"Ash will pick you up. I'm taking Zane and Jonah to the hospital. Jonah's been stabbed. We'll meet you at Zane's as soon as the doctor fixes them," Storm said, hurrying everyone out the door.

Zane took out his phone. Storm pressed a cloth against his shoulder, Jonah looked at him. "Don't tell anyone I've been stabbed. Bird will never shut up."

Zane smiled and dialed his Pollyanna, "Hi, sweetheart, I'm not going to make it tomorrow. Willow's father-in-law found us, so we have to get the hell away from here."

"Did you get hurt?"

"No, sweetheart. I'm fine."

"Zane, I can hear it in your voice."

Storm was looking at him in the rearview mirror, and Jonah was shaking his head at him. Zane shut his eyes and leaned his head back against the seat. "Yes, I was shot in the shoulder, but I'm fine. Storm is taking me to the hospital."

"Put him on the phone."

"Pollyanna wants to talk to you," he said, handing Storm the phone.

"Storm, tell me the truth. What is going on? I want to know everything, even if it's terrible. Tell me."

"He's fine. Once we get the bullet out, he'll be even better."

"Don't get smart, Storm."

"Sorry."

"Who else got hurt?"

Jonah was shaking his head. Storm ignored him. He didn't want Polly to catch him lying. "Jonah, he was stabbed in the side."

"Tell her not to tell Bird," Jonah shouted. "My sister is worse than any mother."

"Jonah doesn't want Bird to know. She went into labor today."

"I won't say anything. Put Zane back on the phone. Zane, I'm flying to Alaska."

"No, sweetheart, we are leaving as soon as the doctor takes the bullet out and sews up Jonah."

"Where are you going?"

"To my house. I'll call you when I get there and let you know what's going on."

"Zane, you better tell me what the hell the doctor says about your stupid bullet hole, and I'm serious. You can't go around getting shot anymore. You have responsibilities now. You have to take care of yourself. I'll talk to you tomorrow." Polly couldn't believe she almost told him about the baby. She had to hurry and hang up the phone.

"She hung up on me. That was a strange phone call. Polly said I better not get shot anymore because I have responsibilities. What do you make of that?"

"Sounds to me like someone is pregnant," Jonah said, leaning back and closing his eyes. His pain was excruciating. He looked over at Zane, who was looking at him as if he said something crazy. "I was kidding. Fuck, Zane, take a breath. Before you pass out."

Storm pulled into the airport and got out. "I'll be right back," he said. He took Ruby from Willow and rushed them both to the jet. Rhys followed with the suitcases. "We'll see you tomorrow at Zane's house."

9

Polly paced the floor, debating whether or not to tell Zane about the baby. *What if he gets himself killed? I don't want to tell Zane he has to quit his job. He'll blame the baby and me forever. Killian still works, and he has children. What the hell am I supposed to do?* Polly heard a noise and turned her head. She screamed her head off. A man stood at her window, looking in at her. She ran to her bedroom and got her gun, as she called nine-one-one. She had to take care of her baby. Polly knew her house was locked up, but what if he broke the window to get inside. She was in her closet when she heard the sirens. When the doorbell went off, she came out of the closet.

"Slow down, and tell me again," the police officer said.

"Listen, a man was standing right there outside the window," Polly said, pointing at the kitchen window. "I screamed and ran to my room and got my gun."

"Let me see your gun."

"You are not getting my gun. I have a carry permit."

"I hope the hell you don't shoot yourself."

"What the fuck does that mean. I am a crack shot. If I see

the bastard again, I'll shoot his fucking ass. I didn't call you out here to lecture me about my gun. Are you going to look around to see if you can find him?"

"There are two officers out there right now. You famous people, bring this on yourselves. You want all the fame, but you don't like what goes with it. Plus, your gate was open."

Polly looked at the cop like he was crazy. "That is a brand new gate. It was replaced because the other gate kept opening. Now I believe someone has been opening the gate all along. No telling how long this person has been watching me." Polly had to make a choice right now. Either she let this guy run her from her house, or she takes a stand. She turned and looked at the policeman. "Do you happen to know anyone I can hire to be my bodyguard?"

The policeman shook his head, "Why don't you call some of your friends and see what company they use. I don't know any bodyguards."

"Okay, I'll take care of it. Thank you, officer, for nothing. You can leave now. I'll lock up."

"There isn't anything we can do if we don't see the man. I'm sorry if you think I'm not doing my job, but I've done all that can be done without finding anyone on your property. We'll do drive-bys and check on you."

Polly wanted them out of there so she could make a plan. She would kill the bastard herself. If she became too scared, she would leave. The more she thought of that, the better it sounded. *I can't leave my house every time someone scares me. I have a child to take care of. I'll have to find a bodyguard. I can't tell Zane either. He's been shot so he can't do anything. This is my problem. I have to work it out somehow.*

"Be sure to lock up after we leave. Do your cameras still work?"

"Yes, I forgot to check my cameras. Let me look at them." Polly hurried over to the television, and the camera wouldn't come on. She looked at her computer and nothing. "It won't come on. I wonder why it isn't working."

"Let me check your wires out; maybe they came loose." Two minutes later, he came back in, shaking his head. I'm going to leave a couple of men here. Your wires have been cut."

Polly had chills from the top of her head to her feet. "Someone cut the wires on my cameras. What about the house alarms?"

"They've all been cut. I'll leave the men here until you can get a bodyguard and someone out here to get your cameras and house alarm going again."

"I'll start calling around tonight." Polly was terrified now. "I wonder how long they've been cut. My niece was here with me last month. Do you think he was watching us then?"

"I don't know. You need to ask your alarm company why they never noticed your alarms were disconnected."

"Oh, believe me, they'll hear from me tonight. Thank you for letting two men stay here with me. They can stay inside. I would feel much safer if they are inside."

"Okay, I'll tell them what you said."

Polly turned and went into her room. There is no way she would let this bastard scare her. She was going to hunt him down tonight and every night until she found him. She wanted to call Zane, but she isn't and never has been a woman who has to lean on a man to take care of things for her.

Zane felt as if his shoulder was on fire. He should have listened to the doctor and not used his arm. He somehow got an infection in his shoulder. He picked up his phone and called Pollyanna. It's been a week since he got shot.

Polly answered on the third ring, "Zane, I was becoming worried about you. How are you?"

"I should be as good as new in a few days. I didn't listen to the doctor and got an infection in my arm. I'm calling to let you know I'll be there tomorrow. I've decided I need to take some time off."

"Zane, are you sure you're able to travel?"

"Yes, I've already asked the doctor. If you are able, you can pick me up at ten tomorrow."

"Yes, I'm able. I can't wait to see you. I miss you so much. Is everyone still at your house?"

"Yes, they'll be here until Willow's ex-father-in-law is behind bars or dead. Sweetheart, I have to go now. I love you."

"I love you too, bye." Polly had a problem. *What should I do about my bodyguard? Should I send him home until Zane leaves? I can't do that. What if the guy shows up? Zane can't fight because of his arm. I'm sure Zane won't let me walk the grounds at night hunting for the guy we know is still out there. I can see him on the cameras. He's dressed all in black with a hood and his face covered up.* Polly was thinking about this problem when her bodyguard came into the room.

"Polly, I've locked everything up. Let me know if you go back outside."

"Okay." Polly felt a little guilty for lying to Pete every night, but she wasn't going to let this crazy man get by with tormenting her. All she had to do was take his face mask off, and she would know who was behind all this crap. Her phone rang, and she answered it automatically.

"Hello." No one was there. It's just as she thought it would be. He started calling her at ten at night and called her four times during the night. Polly didn't dare turn her phone off. She might need it, and sometimes it takes a while to turn back on. "I know you are there, so why don't you say something, you chicken bastard." Polly heard him laugh, and she became scared. Maybe tonight, she wouldn't go outside. Then she heard a strange noise at her bedroom window. She jumped up from the chair she was sitting on. *Should I look out the window?* She decided she would tell her bodyguard about the noise, and he could check it for her.

Polly walked into every room in her house, and she couldn't find her bodyguard. Maybe it was Pete outside. She got her gun and used the flashlight on her phone, and walked around the house. She discovered her bodyguard on the ground outside her window, with a knife in his back. Polly wanted to scream, but she didn't because she felt that was what the man wanted. He tried to scare her to death. Pete was barely breathing. She had to get him some help. She dialed nine-one-one and told them what was going on.

"Should I try taking the knife out of his back?"

"No, leave it where it is. The police are on their way. I also have an ambulance. It should be there in a few minutes."

"I'm afraid he's still out there somewhere," Polly whispered to the woman on the other end of the line.

"You should go lock yourself in the house, and wait there for the police."

"I can't leave Pete out here alone."

"At least put your back to the house. That way, you won't have to look behind you. I'll stay on the line with you."

"Thank you, but I have someone I need to call.

10

Zane had to get some sleep. He felt like he hadn't slept at all since he'd gotten shot. He walked into his bathroom and took one of the sleeping pills the doctor gave him. He was knocked out to the world around him three minutes later. He didn't hear his phone ringing. He had no idea that a man was watching every move Polly made or that he decided to take Polly with him on this night. He didn't know Polly shot at the man and missed or that the man struck her on the side of the head hard enough to cause serious injury.

Zane didn't know any of that until he tried calling Polly to see where she was. He was at the airport. He hailed a taxi to take him to Polly's house. When he got there, his heart almost stopped beating. The place was crawling with cops. "What the hell is going on here?"

One of the police turned around and looked at him. "Do not cross the yellow tape."

"Go screw yourself! I asked what the hell is going on. Polly! He shouted at the top of his lungs."

"I'm sorry, do you know Pollyanna Devlin?

"Yes, I fucking know her. Where the hell is she?"

"If you want answers from me then you will talk to me with more respect than that!" the officer barked. Wanting to get information, Zane reluctantly bit back his response. "We had a call from her last night. She said someone stabbed her bodyguard, and she had her gun. She said she was going to kill that bastard who has been tormenting her. We found her gun out beside the body of the bodyguard. Someone has been terrorizing her."

"Why didn't she tell me she needed a bodyguard?" Zane looked at his phone. He had a missed call from Polly last night. "Is she in the house?"

"No, sir, she's missing—the man who has been stalking her must have taken her with him. We've searched the house and the area. What time did she call you last night?"

Zane looked at his phone. "It was at eleven fifteen."

"Yes, that would be when she called and reported this. She didn't know her bodyguard had died."

"Can you start from the beginning and tell me what the hell is going on?"

Polly called us out here because she saw someone looking into her window. That's when we found all of her wires had been cut to her cameras and the house alarm. We left two officers here for two days until she found a bodyguard. Polly was frightened someone was going to kill her. She said someone was paid to kill her. She didn't know if he was the guy or not."

"Why didn't she call me if she needed help?"

"It looks like you've had your own problems going on," the officer said, pointing at Zane's arm.

∽

Zane had a frown on his face. He had to think. He didn't hesitate even a second. He began to dial the numbers on the phone of people he wanted here to help him. "I need you to come to Polly's in Tennessee as soon as possible. She's been kidnapped. I think it might be the guy who was hired to kill her. Don't tell Missy. We don't need to upset her."

"I thought your shoulder was inflamed."

"I don't give a damn about my shoulder. I'm going to call Brinley. Have the best specialist you can find out here. I need some fingerprints. Ash, only bring the best with you."

"We'll find her. Don't worry."

"I should have been here with her. Pollyanna knew someone was after her. She must have thought I was too busy to help. She was frightened. I told her I couldn't come because we had to keep Willow safe. My God, my Pollyanna was frightened, and I canceled my time with her."

"You can't blame yourself. The sooner I get off this phone, the sooner we can get there. I'll bring all the people we need."

∼

The first person to show up was Storm. "What are you doing here?"

"I'm going to help you find Polly. Ash and the others will be here in about thirty minutes. That will give us time to get our thoughts together."

"Okay, if this is Chester's guy, he took his sweet time getting around to doing what he was hired to do. On the other hand, if it's a stalker, hopefully, he loves Polly so much he's just staring at her. I'm going to make some coffee."

Zane paced up and down the living room. Something was bothering him, and he couldn't put his finger on what the hell it was. He walked into the kitchen, where Storm poured them a cup of coffee. "What if he is the hired killer? What's taken him so long to get around to killing her? Maybe he was in jail or somewhere else, and he couldn't get here until now."

There was a knock at the door, and Zane heard Brinley call out. She had her computer ready to set up. Lucas and Skye walked in behind her, followed by Ash, and Rowan walked in behind him.

"Please tell me Missy doesn't know about Pollyanna."

"Missy doesn't know. Stop worrying. Skye and Lucas are going to get the fingerprints. But I bet you he had gloves on the entire time." The policeman pulled in with his tires screaming. They all stood and watched as the angry officers came into the house.

"What the hell is going on here? Why are all of these people here? This is a crime scene."

"I'm Brinley Cooper, FBI Special Agent."

Skye stepped forward, "Skye Ryan, FBI Special Agent."

Lucas stood next to his wife, Skye, "Lucas Ryan, DEA Special Agent."

"Ash Beckwith, Navy Seal Special Investigations."

"Rowan Scott, Navy Seal Special Investigations, Washington DC."

The officers looked at Zane, waiting for him to say something.

"Zane Taylor, Director at DEA Special Investigations."

"Well, then it seems you all got this under control." He turned when he heard footsteps behind him.

"Sorry, I'm late," said a beautiful woman dressed as a homeless street person.

"What's your name?"

"Who wants to know?"

"Officer Michael Strand."

"FBI Special Agent Julia Sparrow. Undercover."

"Have we ever arrested you?"

"Yes, you have. I beat the crap out of a man who was

beating a helpless child. I went to jail and he went on his way. When I got out of jail, the child was in the hospital. I hunted the man down. He laughed in my face when he told me he had to beat the kid again." She looked at Skye. "If I can't find where she belongs, I'll bring her home with me."

Skye nodded once.

"We'll take our leave. Call me if you find Polly."

"You mean, when we find Polly," Zane said, staring the man down.

The officer nodded. "These guys look like they would shoot anyone who gets in their way," the other officer whispered as they left the house.

"Yep, my thoughts exactly."

~

POLLY KNEW SHE WAS ALIVE, but she couldn't open her eyes or move her body. She remembered being hit but nothing after that. She thought she must have vomited because she could smell it. Then everything went black again.

She could feel someone hurting her. *Am I being raped? What's happened to me? Stop hurting me. Why can't I open my eyes? Did I get into an accident? Someone help me.* It went like this for a week before Polly could open her eyes.

"Finally, I thought you would die before I could kill you. Your friend Chester hired me, but you probably figured that out by now. I would have finished it before now, but I went to jail for beating my ex-girlfriend. Hell, I left her for dead. I was surprised when they arrested me and said I beat her. Can you imagine what I felt when they told me she was still living? I won't make that mistake again."

Polly couldn't understand what he was saying. She tried to focus on his words, but she couldn't stay awake. Two days later, she was still sleeping. Charles shook her and poured water on her face. He wanted to get this job finished; people were sniffing around. The guy at the bar said they were federal agents. Charles didn't want to kill her while she was sleeping, but he had no choice. He took his knife and stabbed her twice. If that didn't kill her, then she must be a witch. He was finished with her, and this State, he wanted to get back to California.

Zane walked the back alleys asking people if they had seen the man in the picture. Lucas finally got one set of prints. The guy was from Los Angeles. His name is Charles Smoot. He's spent the last eight months in the L. A county Jail. Now he's here, and Zane was going to kill him. The sleazy apartment down this alley was rented by the day or by the hour, whatever you needed. Zane and Ash walked up and down these back alleys hammering on the doors since six in the morning. His shoulder was killing him, but he ignored it as long as his infection didn't come back. He took his antibiotics every day as the doctor at the hospital told him to. He ended up at the hospital here in Nashville four days ago. Ash threatened to kill him if he didn't go. He found out that it was pretty bad and promised he would take care of his shoulder and not use his arm.

He pounded on the door of a place he knew had to be a crack house by the person who walked inside. No one answered, so he beat the door again and again until it was opened.

"What the fuck do you want?" the person who answered the door said.

"I want to know if you've seen this guy?

"I am not a fucking snitch. Get the hell away from here."

Zane grabbed him by his filthy shirt with his good arm and threw the guy against the wall. "You listen to me, you son of a bitch! Look at this picture, and tell me if you've seen him."

Another guy was walking inside and glanced at them. He looked at the picture. "He's in that room at the end of the alley."

Zane threw the other guy away from him as he and Ash went to the end of the alley. He didn't bother knocking. He kicked once and the door splintered as it flew open. Then he saw his Pollyanna. She laid on the ground in a pool of blood. Zane roared so loud the walls shook. He dropped to his knees as Ash called for an ambulance. Zane felt her neck for a pulse. He couldn't find anything. He knew he was freaking out, but he was desperate for her to be alive. "Pollyanna baby, please wake up, sweetheart, please wake up."

"Move out of the way and let me check her. Zane, get the fuck out of the way. I need to see if she's still alive." Ash gently turned her over. He tried finding a pulse. "Move out of my way Zane. How can I do anything with you blocking my path? She has a pulse, she's alive!" Ash wiped his arm across his eyes, where a few tears fell. "Polly's lost a lot of blood. Let's see if we can find where the blood is coming from."

Zane pulled her shirt up. There were two knife holes between her shoulders. He took off his tee-shirt and pressed it against the knife wounds to keep more blood from leaving her body. He heard the ambulance and picked her up. Zane held her against him, not knowing tears ran down his face. The ambulance and the police came to a screeching halt in front of Zane. He carried her to the ambulance and crawled in back with her. "Let's get the fuck out of here."

"Sir, you'll have to get out. No one is allowed to ride with us."

"I said, let's get the fuck out of here." Zane closed his eyes and took a deep breath, "I'll stay out of your way. She has two knife wounds between her shoulders, and her head has a large bump. The entire side of her head looks like the kidnaper hit her with a cast-iron skillet."

The EMT talked to the hospital as he hooked Polly up with a drip. He could see by checking her she was dehydrated. He had everything done before Zane knew what he was doing. Then he cut her shirt all the way up, so it fell from the front of her. He got to work on her wounds. He checked them as a doctor on the other end of the phone told him what to do. He wiped her wound with antiseptic and cleaned the dirt from around the wounds.

"Can you tell me how long it's been since she was stabbed? I want to catch the bastard who did this to her."

"I'm not allowed to tell the family members anything. But screw it, it was between this morning and last night. She's lucky the wounds aren't as deep as we thought. I don't know if there is anything damaged. Plus, I don't know how bad her head injury is. I ask myself why she's still unconscious." He looked at Zane, "I'm sorry, I pray she heals fast. I love her singing."

"Thank you, I hope she heals fast as well."

"It's almost like he didn't want to see her face when he stabbed her, so he turned her over. Which is probably what saved her life."

They pulled into the hospital, and the staff made Zane go to the waiting area. He sat there for two hours then his friends walked in. Skye sat down and took his hand. "I'm sorry I wanted to save him for you, but I had no choice; I had to kill him."

"What are you talking about?"

"Charles Smoot, I killed him. He didn't give me a choice. I confronted him, and he charged me with a knife."

"I hope you kicked the hell out of him before he died."

"I knew you would want that, so I kicked him until Lucas made me stop."

"Good. I'm glad you killed the bastard."

"How's your shoulder?"

"Ash made a doctor check it. It'll be fine. I had to hold her close for just a little while." Zane leaned back and closed his eyes.

"I know."

When he opened them again, all of his friends were there. He sat up straight when he saw a doctor come into the waiting room.

"Polly's going to make it. She still hasn't woken up, but the stab wounds didn't harm anything. The baby wasn't injured either. Now we wait for her to wake up."

Zane sat there with his mouth open. *Did he say the baby? I'm going to be a father.* He looked at Lucas and then Skye, who cried openly. "Thank you, doctor. Did you say the baby?"

"Yes, Polly's at least four months pregnant. Congratulations."

"Thank you. Can I see Pollyanna?"

"Yes, you can see her. But only for a little while. You should go home and take a shower and get some rest. Then when you come back, and Polly wakes up, you can tell her I spilled the beans about the baby."

11

Polly felt as if something was wrong. She lay there in bed, trying to remember what happened to her. She could hear people talking. Who in the world would be speaking in her bedroom? She felt herself going back to sleep and went with it.

Zane sat in the hospital room talking to Polly about everything he could think of. All his friends went home. He told her about when he was around three-years-old. His mother went somewhere and forgot she had a toddler waiting at home for her. The Spanish lady who lived next door heard him crying and took him to her house, "Can you imagine Pollyanna? I cried my eyes out when my mother came back a month later. She beat me for going to the neighbor's house. She was a bitch. When she took me from my grandfather, it was because he wouldn't give her money. I remember when my grandfather found me, I couldn't understand him. I had forgotten how to speak English. He had to teach me how to speak English again. I went to a private school to learn what I should have already known. I couldn't read or write. I was big for my age, and the other kids thought it was funny to make fun of me. I don't want you to worry about our baby. I'm going to be the best father for him or her. I'll love my child like no one has ever loved a child. I know how it feels when no one loves you, my baby will never know that feeling."

Polly wished she could open her eyes. She listened as Zane talked to her, poor baby boy. If his mother ever shows her face around her, Polly swore to herself she would beat her ass with a belt. Polly knew Zane wouldn't have told her any of this if he knew she could hear him. He knew they were having a baby. Polly tried touching her tummy so she could let her baby know they would be alright now.

When Zane woke up, Polly's hands were on her stomach. *She must be thinking about our baby. I wonder if I can talk her into marrying me and moving to California.*

"She's still not awake?"

Zane opened his eyes, and Rowan stood in the doorway. "What are you doing here?"

"I came to see how everything was. Has the doctor said anything about her not waking up?"

"No, he said when her body is ready to wake up, she'll wake up. I'm scared they'll want to move her somewhere else. I wish I could take her to California. At least she would be near family. Does Missy know what's going on?"

"Yes, she was getting worried when you and Polly didn't answer your phones. So Piper told her. She'll be here tonight."

Zane looked away. He needed a shower, and he needed to shave. He's had the same clothes on for three days. But he was afraid to leave Polly. What if she woke up? He needed to be here. He looked at Rowan. "Could you go to Polly's and get my duffel bag? It's in the entryway. I haven't put anything away."

"Of course, I can. Give me Polly's address and house key.

Is there anything else you need? How about if I stop and get you something to eat?"

"Sure, can you get me some grilled chicken and steamed vegetables? Do you know what I really want? I'm going to get something else. I'll take a cheeseburger and fries, with a large chocolate milkshake."

Rowan laughed, "Okay, I'll get myself the same thing."

"Did you know Pollyanna is pregnant? I don't know what I'm going to do about my job. I'm probably going to live here if she doesn't move to California with me. I love her so much. I'm a stupid ass, sorry about thinking you were crazy the way you mooned over Piper."

"I don't remember you calling me crazy."

"No, I didn't say it to your face. I just used to think it all the time."

Rowan laughed, "I accept your apology. I'll return as soon as possible."

Polly thought the cheeseburger meal sounded good.

The next thing she remembered was smelling Zane's food. He was going on and on about how good it was. Polly thought that was funny, and she giggled.

Zane stopped chewing. He looked at Rowan, "Did Pollyanna giggle?"

"Yes, I believe she did."

"Sweetheart, can you hear me? Pollyanna, can you hear me? She must have heard me talking about my food and thought it was funny." He pushed the button, and a nurse came in.

"What did she do?"

"She giggled. I was eating my meal and telling Rowan how good it was, and Pollyanna giggled."

The nurse walked over to Polly, "Are you finally going to wake up? It's about time you woke up. Polly, open your eyes. I can see by looking at your monitors that you are joining us.

Can you hear me?" The nurse took Polly's hand. "Squeeze my hand if you can hear me."

"That's wonderful. Can you open your eyes for me? That's okay, you can try again in a bit. I'm going to call your doctor while you talk to this man of yours."

As soon as the nurse dropped Polly's hand, Zane picked it up. He kissed the back of her hand. He kissed each finger, then he kissed her lips. "Can you hear me, sweetheart?" Polly squeezed his hand. Zane would have cried if Rowan wasn't there.

"Zane, I'll see you later."

"Rowan, thank you for coming."

"Hey, you're my friend. I'm glad I came. I'll let everyone know Polly's starting to wake up. The first call will go to Missy."

"Thank you."

∽

Polly opened her eyes, it was dark, but she could see Zane sleeping in the hospital chair. She watched him until he opened his eyes and saw her. They gazed into each other's eyes. She patted the bed beside her. Polly smiled at Zane. "Hey."

"Hey yourself." Zane sat next to her and pulled her into his arms. "I have to tell you, Polly; this scared the hell out of me. I love you so much, sweetheart. How do you feel?"

Polly's throat hurt. She didn't know if she could talk or not. "I hurt everywhere."

Zane wanted to kill that man again for what he did. He kissed Polly on her forehead. "I'm sorry I wasn't there. You shouldn't have been alone. I'm sorry."

"Zane. You have nothing to be sorry for. It wasn't up to

you to keep me safe. I'm the one who said I didn't need you to guard me. How is my bodyguard?"

"He didn't make it."

"Oh my God, that bastard killed him. Zane, you have to catch him."

"He's dead sweetheart, he'll never hurt another person. Do you have something to tell me?"

Polly frowned, trying to think. Then she smiled. "I remember hearing you talking about our baby. I wanted to wait to tell you. I didn't want you to think, because I was pregnant, that you had to stay with me. I was going to tell you about the baby when you came back. Because I know you love me." Polly could feel her eyes starting to close.

"You and I are going to be terrific parents. No matter where we live. Close your eyes and get some sleep. Missy will be here later today. You have to save your energy for her visit."

"I can't wait to see her," Polly said with her eyes closed.

Zane borrowed the shower in Polly's room. He shaved and dressed in clean clothes. He was getting ready to leave the bathroom when he heard someone trying to stifle their crying. He walked out and saw Missy with her back turned, trying not to cry.

"Hey sweetie, it's going to be okay. Pollyanna is going to be alright. I talked to her, and so will you, as soon as she wakes up."

"I should have moved to Tennessee with her. She wouldn't have been alone."

"Missy, come over here so I can talk to you," Polly said, looking at her niece. "Honey, it wouldn't have mattered if you were with me. I'm sure he would have hurt both of us. I'm so thankful you were not with me. I have something to tell you."

"Is it good news?"

"It's the best news ever. Zane and I are having a baby."

Missy sat down and cried.

"What's the matter, sugar plum?"

"He could have killed the baby."

"But he didn't. The doctor told me the baby is fine. So I was thinking I'm going to have to move to California so you and her daddy can help me with her."

"Do you already know it's a girl?"

"No, I just feel that she's a baby girl."

"We are going to have so much fun. Polly, when do you have to go home?"

"Not for a while."

"How long do you get to stay?"

"I was thinking about changing colleges and moving here, but now that I know you are going to move to California, I'll go back home and not miss my classes. I'm so excited. Where are you going to live?"

"She'll live with me," Zane said, looking at his Pollyanna. "Pollyanna, you know how much I love you. I never want to live without you. Will you do me the honor of becoming my wife?"

Missy shouted yes before Polly could say anything. Polly looked at her, and both of them burst out laughing. Tears ran down Polly's face when she looked at Zane, who had a grin on his face. "Yes, I'll marry you, Zane Taylor. I love you so much. I don't want a life without you in it." She heard crying, and she looked at the doorway. Three nurses stood there crying.

Zane reached her in a heartbeat. He scooped her up and kissed her. He heard applause, so he raised his head. "You've made me the happiest man in the world." He looked at the nurses. "When can Pollyanna leave the hospital?"

"Zane, she just woke up this morning. There are lots of tests the doctor has lined up for Polly. Starting right now. We are going to wheel her down and do a scan of her head. She was asleep for a long time. I'm sure everything is good, we just have to do these tests. In fact, we have more tests after that. You should go do something. Come back this afternoon. We will do an ultrasound of the baby and you can see your baby moving around."

12

"We are having a girl. Shay, she's so special. That bastard left me for dead. He could have killed my baby."

"But he didn't. Let's focus on everything that is going good for you. Now, when are you moving?"

"When I'm able to move around. I can't wait to get out of this hospital, even though I love the nurses here. They are amazing."

"Why are you moving?"

"Because Zane lives in Los Angeles and Missy lives there also. I don't want to be away from Zane. I now know what is important in my life: Zane, Missy, and the baby. I don't care where I live as long as he's with me."

"Where is he?"

"He took Missy to the airport."

"When are you getting married?"

"When we get back to Los Angeles. I hope you can come to the wedding?"

"I wouldn't miss it. Let me know as soon as you know the

date, and I'll plan around it. I'm so happy you're awake. All of your friends were worried about you."

"I know. I have boxes of get-well cards. Thank you for taking time out of your tour to come and visit me."

"I'm so happy you're going to be alright." Shay hugged Polly and smiled. "You should ask Bird to sing her new song at your wedding."

"Does she sing in front of people now?"

"She doesn't like to. But she'll do it for you because her new song is amazing. I want her to record it herself. Her voice is magical. Ask her."

Polly laughed, "Okay, I will."

"Call me as soon as you have the date. I hate leaving you without Zane being here."

"It's okay, I'm going to sleep. I'll probably sleep until Zane gets back."

∼

ZANE WALKED into Polly's room, and it was empty. He walked to the nurse's station to see where she was. "Can you tell me where Pollyanna is?"

"The doctor ordered more scans of her head. She said her head hurt, and her eyes were blurry. I'm sure everything will be fine. We are just taking precautions."

"Where is her doctor?

"He's seeing other patients. As soon as he gets the scans, I'll tell him you want to talk to him."

"I want to talk to him now."

The nurses knew when Zane Taylor wanted something, it was better to give it to him because he wouldn't leave you alone until he got what he wanted. "Don't tell anyone I told you this. He's in the doctor's lounge. They are having a going-away get-together for a resident doctor who is transferring to another State."

"Point me in the right direction. I'm going to talk to him before Pollyanna comes back." Zane walked to the doctor's lounge. He had to knock to get in. Then he lied. "Sorry, I'm late."

"Who are you?"

"Doctor Taylor. Who are you?"

"I'm sorry, I have to ask everyone who comes in here. We don't want people sneaking in for the party."

"Of course you don't." Zane spotted the doctor and walked over to him. He didn't say a word. He didn't have to. His body language said it all. He was pissed. This man should be with Pollyanna. He shouldn't be here drinking wine. He looked around and couldn't believe how much alcohol was already drunken. The wine bottles were lined up on the table. Zane took his phone out and took pictures. "Who drives these people home? Does any of them have surgery today?"

"Hello, Doctor Mill's. I would rather you be with Pollyanna instead of in here drinking. Now I don't want you to see her at all. It's ten in the morning, and you're all consuming alcohol. You're fired." Zane shook his head. He took out his phone and called an acquaintance.

"Hello, this is Doctor Strong. How can I help you?"

"Hi Frankie, this is Zane Taylor. I need you to refer me to a great doctor in Tennessee."

"Zane, wow, I didn't think I would ever hear from any of you again. So tell me why you need a great doctor."

Zane told her about Pollyanna and everything that is going on with her. "I went hunting for her doctor. He was in the doctor's lounge getting drunk with all the other doctors."

"I know someone who specializes in head injuries. I'll call him now. I heard he was on vacation. I might not hear from him for a day or two. The only way to know is to call him now. If he's available, I'll give him your phone number."

"Thank you, Frankie. Is there anyone you want me to say hi to?"

"Nope, no one. He's the one who left."

"Okay, thank you for helping me."

"I hope Jason gets back to you. Goodbye, Zane."

Thirty minutes later, Zane got the phone call. "This is Dr Jason Burks. Do not let anyone do surgery on her. I'll be there as soon as I can get there, that will be in about forty-five minutes. Fire her doctor she has now. Any doctor that drinks on the job needs to be fired."

"Already done. Thank you, Dr Burks. I'll be here." Zane couldn't believe the doctor called him back so fast. Now he needed to wait for Pollyanna to get back to her room. He called Ash and filled him in on what was going on. "Frankie Strong called a friend who happened to be a specialist on head injuries."

"Frankie Strong," Ash whispered, "I'll be sure not to let Storm know about that."

"I asked her if she wanted to give anyone a message, and she said no, he's the one who left."

"She must have forgotten that she was always firing him. She thought he would walk over to her uncle's again, but that was the last time for him. When she fired him for the fourth time, he said he wanted someone else to be brought in, and he wanted to be sent far away. Frankie thought Storm would trade places with Austin again, who was at her uncle's home guarding her mother." Ash explained. "But he changed places with Marc, in New York. I think Storm was burned once, and he doesn't want to get too deeply involved with anyone."

"Hey, I'm just thankful she got Dr Burks for me. I'll let you know what the doctor says. I'll talk to you later."

Zane stood up as they rolled Pollyanna's bed back into her room. "Hey sweetheart, I hear you have a headache."

"Zane, you don't have to stay here with me all the time. I'm sure you have more important things to do than sit here watching me."

"Sweetheart, I have a specialist on his way here to see you."

"Why?"

"Because your head hurts, and your eyes are blurry. Can you please let me have my way this time?"

Polly smiled, "You always get your way. I'll be happy to talk to anyone who can help me."

Zane could tell her head hurt. He could see it in her eyes. He fluffed her pillow and looked at her. Polly was sound asleep.

Zane stood looking out the window when Dr Burks walked in. He spotted Zane standing at the window and smiled. He wondered if this was the same Zane Taylor he knew. *Well, he looks the same as he did in college, just bigger with more muscle.* "Hello Zane, I see you haven't changed."

Zane turned around, ready to fight. "Jason Burks, long time no see. The last time I saw you was when you and my fiancée were in bed together. So you are the Doctor Burks Frankie told me about?"

"Damn it, Zane, if you would have listened to me explain everything to you, you would have known I did you a favor. Tracy was cheating on you with every male in our dorm. I tried telling you, but you wouldn't listen to me. So I thought I would show you. I called you and told you I had something to show you. Well, that's what it was. Tracy, the whore, sleeping with your best friend. I took the chance you wouldn't speak to me ever again, but that was a chance I took because I knew you would marry her if I didn't do something. I wondered if you were the same Zane Taylor." Jason turned around to the bed where Polly was. She was staring at him. He smiled. She didn't smile back.

"Zane, I'm going to thank this man. If he hadn't slept with Tracy, then I would have never met you."

"There is that," Zane said, walking to the bed. "Pollyanna Devlin, this is Jason Burks. He's the doctor I told you about. Jason, this woman is my life. Take great care of her."

Jason looked at Polly. "You have a blood clot on the optic nerve. It's putting pressure on the optic disc, which is causing it to swell. It's causing stress on the nerve. We need to operate and remove the blood clot."

"Is it dangerous? I mean, could I go blind if you don't remove it?"

"You would go blind, plus your headaches will only get worse. The sooner we take care of it, the better chance you will have of not having permanent nerve damage."

"Okay, when can we get it done?"

"I've already taken care of all that. Surgery is scheduled for three this afternoon. It won't be a long surgery, and you should be as good as new afterward."

"Thank you, doctor. I'll be glad for this pressure in my head to be gone."

"I'll see you in surgery, Miss Devlin." He looked at Zane, "Zane, it was nice seeing you."

Zane nodded his head, then he stepped forward. "Jason, I'm sorry I didn't listen to you. I was a college kid who thought he was in love, and now I know it was lust, and I know why Tracy knew so much about sex. I'm damn happy I didn't marry her."

13

Zane was waiting when they moved Pollyanna back into her room. She had a bandage over one eye. Jason followed them in. He looked at Zane. She'll be as good as new in a few days. I was looking at her charts. She got beat up pretty bad."

"Yeah, she did. We found her just in time. I heard you were on vacation."

"Yeah, my family is waiting for me to get back to them. Zane, how long has it been since you've seen Tracy?"

"I haven't seen her since that night. Why do you ask?"

"Her oldest son could be your twin."

"What are you talking about?"

"I saw her last year, and she wasn't happy that I ran into her. She has a husband and three kids. The oldest looks like you. I don't know if he is yours or if he just looks like you. I feel us seeing each other at this time was fate. Maybe you want to take a look at this boy."

"Who did she marry?"

"I don't know if she's married, but his name is Sean

Palmer. I think he runs a construction crew in Las Vegas, Nevada. I thought you might want to know. Don't worry about Miss Devlin, a friend of mine will take over her care."

"Thank you, Jason, for everything. I'll check this boy out and see how much he looks like me."

"When you go, I want to go with you," Polly whispered.

"I wouldn't want to go anywhere without you, sweetheart. How are you feeling?"

"I feel like someone beat the crap out of me. Have I thanked you for saving me? I'm going to go back to sleep."

"Okay, sweetheart. I'm going to get my laptop out of the car." Zane got down to business right away. The first thing he did was check out Tracy's husband or boyfriend what ever he was. Then Zane pulled up a picture of Tracy's family. Hell, he even got her Facebook pictures. There weren't many of her oldest son, and he was always standing off to himself. Zane zoomed in on the photo. His breathing changed as he looked at the boy. He was the image of Zane when he was younger. Zane added up the years. If this boy was his son, then he was thirteen. He called Austin Sawyer, who was in college with him and Jason. He and Austin both became Navy Seals together.

"Hello."

"Hey, Austin, I have something for you to check out for me."

"Sure, how's Polly?"

"Pollyanna's doing good. As soon as she can get around without being in so much pain. We'll be going home to California and getting married. She had surgery to get rid of a blood clot. Guess who her doctor was?"

"I have no idea."

"Jason Burks."

"How did that go?"

"I thanked him for screwing Tracy. I'm happier than hell I didn't marry her. He also had some information for me. He said her oldest son looked like me. So I got a photo of him. I'm going to send it to you and all the other information I have about her husband. She has three children. Just by looking at their pictures, it would seem that the oldest isn't included in a lot of their photos. Austin, I want to know if this is my son. If I could go, I would, but Pollyanna needs me here with her."

"Zane, I don't need you here right now. This is important. Go see if this boy is your son. Don't wait for me. We don't know how long it will be before I can get around good enough to travel."

Zane looked at Polly, he didn't want to leave her, but he had to find out if this boy belongs to him. "Alright, I'll meet you in Las Vegas, Austin. Can you see if Jonah is free to go? I might need a lawyer."

"I just got his photo. You're right. You'll need Jonah there. There is no way that he is not your son."

"Yeah, that's what I thought as well. I'll see you tomorrow." He looked at Polly, "Here, take a look at this photo. Are you able to see it?"

"Yes, I can see perfect out of the other eye." Polly looked at the boy, wondering what his name was. "He's very handsome, just like his Dad. I wonder what his name is." Polly looked at Zane, "Our baby is going to have a big brother."

Zane sat down. He didn't know what to do. He was a little in shock. "Do you think he's been treated like I was by my mother?"

"No, I don't think that at all. He looks like he's doing fine. The only way we will know for sure is for you to confront her and demand to know why she kept this child from you. Call me right away and tell me all about him."

Zane smiled, "I'll call you ten times a day. I'm going to

miss you so much. Don't try doing anything alone. Call the nurses. In fact, I'll stop by their station and have a talk with them."

He kissed her on the forehead and squeezed her hand in his.

14

"Zane, you can't go in there acting like a fucking crazy father. You need to calm down. You don't know if he's mistreated," Jonah said, pacing in front of Zane and Austin.

"Calm down, Jonah. I'm not going to go rushing in there like a crazy person."

"I know you won't do that. That's what scares me. You're too damn calm. You can't go in there killing anyone. I know you're angry. Hell, I'm angry also. We have to wait until the judge gives us those papers giving you custody of your son."

"Jonah, I know all this. You need to calm down. If the bastard she's living with walks close enough, I'm going to beat the fuck out of him. The bastard hurt my son. Can you believe she named him Taylor? Since that's his last name, we'll have to fix that. Why did you think to check out the hospital?"

Jonah shrugged his shoulders, "He looked sad in his photos. I wondered why he looked sad. So I made a few calls to some old friends who were judges and they emailed me the papers. I'm glad the hospital and social service didn't look at the State those papers came from. He has run away six times. He's been in the hospital from injuries. I'm going to kill the son of a bitch. If he's not home, I'll hunt his ass down. Oh, here she comes."

"Mr. Brewer, here are the papers. I'm happy the boy will no longer be living in that home with his so-called mother. The judge was able to get more information for you. I put those papers in with the others. I thought you might need them soon. I also called my son-in-law. He's a sheriff. He's going to go there with you to make sure there is no trouble."

"Thank you, is he going to meet us there?"

"He's outside right now waiting for you. I pray everything goes good for you. She turned and looked at Zane. Good luck, sir."

"Thank you for everything. We couldn't have gotten this far without you."

She blushed as Zane took her hand, "You're welcome. I'm glad I was still here."

∼

Jonah pulled in behind the Sheriff's car, and the four of them stepped out of the vehicle. One stayed near the vehicle. The sheriff looked at them and knew he wouldn't want to go up against them. He followed them to the front door. And watched as the one in the suit knocked on the door.

"Hello, Tracy. I came to get my son."

"Get out of here. Do you want to start trouble for me?"

"I'm here for no other reason than to get my son. Are you going to get him?"

"I don't know what you are talking about."

"Well, I'll fill you in. I saw Jason Burks. He told me you had a son who looked just like me. So I did a little investigating. Taylor is my son. I have all the papers I need to take him from you. I have full custody. Please call your boyfriend because I'm going to kill the bastard. I have all the hospital records. I have his school records. I have the records from the social service department. You can bring him to me, or I will fucking go in there and get him."

"Be quiet, I told Greg, Taylor's father was dead. You have no right to him. Zane, you need to leave here. You'll cause more trouble for Taylor."

"Who the hell are you talking to?" a large man who looked like he probably drank too much asked. He walked up to stand next to Tracy.

"Zane Taylor, I'm Taylor's father. I've come to take my son away from your fucking ass."

"You said his father died," he accused, looking at Tracy.

"I thought he had died. I'm in shock just as you are."

"You fucking liar. What else did you lie about? Get the fuck off my property, or I'll get you off myself." He got in Zane's face.

Zane smiled. That's what he was waiting for. His fist landed in the guy's face. "Get the fuck away from me, or I will kill you." Zane growled he looked at Tracy, "Get my son, or I'm going to kill this bastard."

"Taylor, get your ass out front. You know Zane, I would have told you about Taylor if you wouldn't have dumped me."

"I found you in bed with my best friend. Then I found out you slept with most everyone in my dorm. So don't try to put the blame on me. You've kept my son from me. I'm taking him with me." Zane felt someone staring at him. He looked behind him, and his son stood there.

"Are you my dad?"

"Yeah, I'm your dad. You'll be living with me from now on. I'm sorry I wasn't here sooner. But I didn't know I had a son. Do you need to get anything?"

"He's not taking one thing from here. I'm glad you're taking the bastard away from here," the man with the busted nose said.

Zane turned and hit him again. "You are lucky I haven't killed you. We got the hospital records and all the other papers that showed how you treated my son."

"Zane," Jonah said, frowning. He saw the look on Zane's face. He backed up so he wouldn't get any blood on his clothes. Zane hit the ass hole twice, both times in the face. Jonah heard the sound of a bone-breaking. The guy fell to the ground, and Taylor kicked him. Then he smiled and walked to the car.

"Don't you want anything? Do you want to tell your mom goodbye?"

"No, I don't want to tell her anything. I don't live in the house with them. I lived in the backyard by myself since I was four. I wasn't allowed to talk to any of them, or Greg would beat me."

Zane turned and looked at Tracy. He roared at the top of his voice. He wished she was a man so he could beat her to death. "My son lived in the backyard while you lived in the house. He was a baby. You put a baby in the backyard to live by himself. You bitch, I wish I had brought one of my lady friends with me to kick your ass." He looked over at the Sheriff, "Did you get all of that?"

"Yes, sir, I'll call it in right now. Have a safe trip home."

"We will. Thank you for coming with us." He looked over at Tracy, "This isn't over."

He looked at his son and put his arm around his shoulders. "You and I are going to do great together. I love you, son. Ever since my friend told me that he saw you and you looked like me, I've wanted to hurry and find you. I'm so happy I have a son."

"I'm glad you're my dad. Do you have other kids?"

"No, but I will have in a few months. I'm getting married. Will you be my best man?" Zane felt himself rushing but he wanted his son to feel like he was part of him. He knew how it felt to have no one love you.

"Yeah, but what if she doesn't like me?"

That broke his heart. He knew his son had known pain and heartbreak the same way he had as a child. He hugged him. "You don't have to worry about that with Pollyanna. She's anxious to meet you. We need to do something about your name."

"How come?"

"Because my last name is Taylor. I'm Zane Taylor soon as we can, we'll change your name to mine. What is your middle name?"

"I don't have a middle name."

"Well, then why don't we think about a middle name for you? Are you hungry?"

"Yeah, I'm starving. How long can I stay with you?"

"You will stay with me forever. You're my son. If I had known about you I would haven't gotten you when you were a baby. I'm sorry for what you had to go through."

"It was alright while I was at school, I got to eat breakfast and lunch there. Don't tell anyone but the girl who lived behind us gave me sandwiches. Where are we going to stop and eat?"

Zane laughed, "These are my friends Jonah Brewer and Austin Sawyer, and Ash Beckham. We'll stop at the in and out burger." Zane watched the boy as he sat in the back with him. He couldn't believe he had a son, a mistreated son who was abused by his mother and her boyfriend. He would make sure they went to jail for this. "What do you like to do, Taylor?"

"I like to listen to music, and I like reading."

"Do you like sports?"

ZANE

"No, I've never played sports. My mom wouldn't let me do any of that stuff. I had a friend where we used to live. He knew I lived in the backyard by myself. He told his mother, and I was taken to a group home for a while. I played baseball there, but I wasn't very good at it. When I got out, we moved across town. Greg and my mom beat me for telling my friend I lived in the backyard, after that, I wasn't allowed to have friends."

"You can have as many friends as you like with me. I never was good at sports either. Ash, the guy driving, played baseball in college. He could give you some pointers if you ever decide you want to play."

"Thank you. Am I really going to live with you forever? What if my mom and Greg come and get me?"

"They can't come and get you, I have full custody. Do you think you'll like living with me?"

"Do I get to live inside the house?"

"You'll not only live inside, but you'll have your own room with a bathroom. You'll get to eat whenever you are hungry. I'll take you to school and sign you in myself. If you don't want to go to a public school, we can find you a private school. I'm so sorry I didn't know about you. I would have taken you if I knew I had a son."

"I didn't know I had a dad either. I'm glad you found me. I was going to kill myself tonight."

The inside of the vehicle got real quiet. Zane could hear his heart speed up inside his chest. It was physically painful. He looked at his son, who was almost as tall as him. "Why were you going to kill yourself?"

"Because Greg said he was going to treat me like I was his little sex toy."

Zane couldn't speak. He has never in his life been this angry. He knew he would be going back to teach fucking

Greg a lesson he would remember forever. He looked at his son, "Has he ever touched you like that?"

"No, he came in my shed once before, my mom's daughter saw him, and she ran out there and screamed at him to leave me alone."

"How old is she?"

"She's eleven."

"Is Greg her father?"

"No, I told her to stay away from Greg. I told her he was weird. She isn't allowed to talk to me, but she sneaks in my shed once in a while."

Ash spoke before Zane had a chance to. They all heard the low growl in his voice, "He's a fucking bastard. He'll pay for everything. That dirty son of a bitch."

Zane tapped his shoulder for him to shut up. "We'll make sure he won't ever touch a child."

"What kind of work do you do," Taylor asked Zane.

"I used to be a DEA agent, but now I'm a high-security bodyguard."

"Do you have to go away for a long time when you work?"

"I'm going to always be available for you every day. Besides, you'll have so many people around you you'll want to hide in your room all the time."

"I won't do that. I like being around people. I was always scared growing up, so I like nice people around me."

"You'll never be scared living with me. I'll make sure of it."

"When I'm a man, I'm going to arrest all the people who are mean to kids."

"I'll help you to achieve that goal." He smiled at his son and ruffled his hair. He needed to get him fed and clothed urgently. "Oh, by the way, we are going to stay at the safe house for a few days. A mother and her child are staying at our house because someone is trying to kill her."

"What is a safe house? Who wants to kill her?"

Zane smiled to himself. He thought that would get his son's interest. "It's her ex-father-in-law. He's in the mob, so she needed someplace safe to stay. My house is very safe. The safe house is where we bring someone people who are hiding from someoneand need to stay in a safe place."

"Where is the safe house?"

"It's not far from our house."

"Is that where Pollyanna is?"

"No, Pollyanna is in Nashville. She's in the hospital."

"Is she sick?"

"She was kidnapped and beaten really bad. She's getting better. It's just going to take some time. When she feels strong enough, she'll move here with us."

"I bet you wish you were there to protect her. Where are the people who took her now?"

"He's dead."

"Did you kill him?"

"No, my friend Skye killed him. Skye is an FBI Special Agent."

"Wow, can I meet her?"

Zane chuckled. "Yes, you'll meet all my friends. I have lots of them."

"Are they all like Skye?"

"Yes, most of them are." Zane thought his son was running out of questions, but he was wrong. They stopped to feed Taylor four times on the way home, and he talked the entire time. Zane thought since Taylor was never able to speak to anyone, he was making up for all those years.

15

Zane knew it was late, but he had to talk to Pollyanna. He let it ring until she answered. "Sweetheart, they mistreated my son."

"Zane, oh no, tell me everything."

"He has had to live in the backyard by himself since he was four. He lived in a shed. Those two are going to hang if I have anything to do with it. Hell, when Taylor was talking to us in the car, I think we all had tears in our eyes. He is so giving. You're going to love him. He's not like a thirteen-year-old boy. He's never had anyone love him. Don't you think it's strange how my life was when I was little and Taylor's life? Sweetheart, Taylor kept walking out the back door, forgetting that he could come into the house, and he didn't live outside anymore. He told us he planned on killing himself tonight because of his mother's boyfriend telling him some sick fucking stuff. It was fate that I saw Jason when I did. My son would have killed himself tonight." Zane pinched the bridge of his nose as the tears fell down his face.

Pollyanna sniffed, "What kind of a fucking mother is she?

I swear when I feel better, I'm going to kick her ass. How could anyone treat a child like that?"

"Yeah, he could barely get to sleep because he was in a big bed. I put him in the room next to mine. He had everyone in the house wanting to murder Greg. I think Ash went back there. I heard him on the phone with Arrow and Brinley. I asked Ash what he planned on doing. He said he has nothing planned. He claimed he was going to visit a friend. I don't believe him, and he's not answering his phone," Zane poured out his soul to Pollyanna. He could no longer hold it all in.

"Zane, concentrate on your son. Take care of him. Take him shopping and buy him everything he wants and needs. He needs you right now. There is nothing you can do here. We'll talk on the phone. I don't want you worrying about me. Send me some photos of the two of you. Talk to him and tell him how much you love him so he understands the baby won't take his place in your heart."

"Thank you for loving me, Pollyanna. I love you so much. I'm going to let you go to sleep now. I'll talk to you tomorrow."

"Goodnight Zane, I love you."

Zane put the phone down, he wanted to murder Greg, but he needed to stay here for Taylor. Tomorrow they would change his name. They decided his name would be Taylor Michael Taylor. Zane knew Taylor didn't want to get rid of his first name since he knew it was a part of his dad, so all they did was add a middle name and put in their last name. He didn't get to sleep until around three and was late waking up. When he walked downstairs, Taylor was up eating breakfast. Warren was there cooking for him. "Warren, what are you doing here?"

"Marc told me about Taylor. I couldn't wait to meet him. And it's a good thing too. This boy is hungry."

"Good morning Taylor. I see you met Warren. He lives with us. Warren took care of my grandfather."

"I know. Warren has been telling me about your grandpa. I'm sorry your mom was mean."

"I guess we have that in common. I think we're lucky we have each other."

Killian walked into the kitchen, "Warren, did you make enough food for me also."

"Yes, Killian, I'll get you a plate."

"You sit down. I'll get my own plate. Who do we have here?"

"Killian, this is my son, Taylor. Son, this is Killian Cooper. He's another Navy Seal buddy of ours. Killian was our Lieutenant."

Taylor beamed at being introduced as Zane's son. He'd never felt wanted like this. "Do you live here too?"

"Only when I have to. I live in Temecula with my wife and kids." He looked at Zane. "Emma will be here in a few minutes. Skye called her and explained a few things to her, and Emma, being how Emma is, has decided to straighten a few people out." They heard the front door open and then voices.

Skye, Emma, and Dakota walked into the room. Zane watched his son and smiled. Taylor looked like he would fall out of his chair. "Taylor, these ladies are Killian's sisters. Skye, I told you about her. Then you have Emma and Dakota."

Taylor smiled, and Emma laughed. "He looks just like you. My God, he's going to break some hearts. Hi Taylor, do you mind if I ask you a few questions?"

"I'll ask the questions," Dakota said. We want to know about Greg. It would seem he's not who he says he is," Dakota explained, looking at Zane.

"What do you mean?"

"Ash called Brinley, and she checked him out. Ash took his photo and sent it to Brinley. She ran it through the database. Greg is running drugs through Mexico, big time. Those girls they have were taken when they were babies. Greg isn't his real name. It's Tony Brown. He's on the ten most wanted list of the FBI. Taylor, do you remember seeing your mother pregnant?"

"No, I don't remember seeing her pregnant. I lived outside in the shed. So I didn't see her much."

"But that was ten years ago. You were only three."

"I lived in the shed, I thought I was four, Dad, but now I remember I was three."

Zane looked at Taylor then he pulled him into his arms. "Did I forget to say I give hugs to the ones I love? So get used to it." He was tearing up.

"Okay."

The ladies looked at each other. In all the years they knew Zane, this is the first time they saw him talk like a man with feelings. Zane has always been so hard, and they didn't realize he could actually have these feelings. Skye wiped tears from her eyes. "What the fuck are you talking about?" she demanded, looking at Taylor.

"Taylor lived in the backyard since he was three. He wasn't allowed to go into the house or talk to anyone who lived in the house. I'll tell you about it later."

"Didn't you hear us? I said we are leaving with Killian, and that bastard will pay for treating someone we love the way he treated Taylor. I know you want to go, Zane, but it's better if you stay here with your son. That way, you won't go to prison for murder."

"I'm not going to argue with you. I know you'll take care of everything for me. Did Ash go there?"

"No, Ash went to the town the babies were stolen from."

Skye looked at Emma, "I swear if he's messed this investigation up, I will wring his fucking neck."

Taylor walked over to Skye, "Can you tell me how to be an FBI agent?"

"You betcha I will. The first thing we need to do is sign you up for martial arts. Zane, you can get started on that."

"Is that what you want to do, Taylor?"

"Yes, when can we sign up?"

"Tomorrow. We have other things to do today."

"We do? What are we going to do?"

"We're going shopping. You have no clothes to wear except what you have on."

"Where are we going to shop?"

"The mall."

"The mall. I've never been to the mall. You're going to have to tell me what to do."

"Have you never been shopping?"

"No. never."

"Well, I'll tell you something, you are going to have a blast. Let's go. Bye ladies, be sure you give it to him and Tracy good."

"We will call you and fill you in. How is Polly doing?"

"She's doing better. They are helping her walk around. Those busted ribs are causing her a lot of pain. But she says she's doing great."

"Have fun shopping," Skye said as she watched Taylor. Then she surprised herself by walking over and hugging him.

16

Polly felt like she was on fire. She didn't want to bother the nurses. She reached for the water when a pain in her neck made her fall back on the bed and moan. A nurse was walking past her door and was in there in an instant.

"What is it, Polly?"

"My neck is hurting me, and I feel like I'm burning up. Maybe I could get a fan or something. I think if I could have a Tylenol and some cold water, I'll be able to sleep."

"I'll get you some fresh cold water. That should help you feel better." The nurse walked closer to Polly and looked closely at her. She touched her forehead. "I'm going to take your temperature." She took Polly's temperature twice, and her vitals "I'll get your water and be right back."

Polly must have taken a nap because when she opened her eyes, Doctor Burks was there, as well as the nurse. "I thought you were on vacation?"

"I am, but I came to town, we rented a cabin out of town, so I thought I would stop by and see how you are doing. The nurse tells me you have a fever."

"That must be why I feel so hot."

"She said your neck hurts."

"I'm sure it's how I slept on my pillow. I'm sure everything is going to be okay. You don't have to worry about me. Go enjoy your vacation."

"I've ordered you some antibiotics."

"Will they hurt my baby if I take them?"

"No, I'm going to have your neck scanned. Just to make sure everything is okay. I don't want you to worry."

"I'm not worried, but I don't want anyone to call Zane if something shows up. He's with his son."

"Is he? So the boy was his."

"Yes, he looks so much like Zane." Polly didn't mention anything about Taylor. He didn't need to know their family business. "How much longer am I going to be in the hospital? I want to get out so I can start my life with Zane and Taylor."

"Well, it all depends on what's going on with you right now. I've already ordered your scan, so they'll be here soon to get you. Tell me if anything else is going on with you. How are your eyes doing?"

"I'm not having any problems with my eyes. I no longer have a headache. It's just my neck. Maybe I have a sore throat. The antibiotics should take care of everything."

The nurse gave Polly some medicine as soon as she got back to her room. Polly fell asleep. Her phone ringing woke her up. She was still sleepy when she answered.

"Hey sweetheart, did I wake you up?"

"I was just dozing. How is Taylor doing?"

"He's great. We went shopping at the mall for most of the day. Now that we know his size, we can order most of his things over the internet. He doesn't like shopping, we have that in common. How are you doing, darling?"

"I'm doing good I'm up walking more often. I'm sure I'll be as good as new in no time. The baby is moving a lot now. I think she wants out of the hospital as much as I do. Are you home now?"

"No. We are still at the safe house. Warren is here with us because the guys are still using my house. No one can get on my property without them knowing about it. If it weren't for the woman and baby, I wouldn't have loaned my home to the Band of Navy Seals. As soon as her father-in-law is taken into custody, they'll move out, and we will move in."

"I hope they catch him soon. That poor woman is trying to keep herself and the baby safe. Zane, I'm going to take a shower. Can I call you back later?"

"Yes, sweetheart. I'll talk to you later. I love you so much."

"I love you too, Zane. I miss you."

∽

ZANE FELT something was off with Polly. He redialed her number, and there was no answer. He called the nurse's station. "This is Zane Taylor. I'm calling about Pollyanna Devlin. I talked to her, and she said she is going to take a shower. I want to know what's going on. How is she doing?"

"She has a fever. We put her on antibiotics. Miss Devlin should be fine by tomorrow. She's getting around much better than when you were here. Doctor Burks says she'll be able to go home soon."

"That's great. I'll be there on Thursday. I'll call her later this evening." Zane hung up the phone and walked outside, looking for Taylor. "Hey, Taylor, do you feel like going somewhere to get something to eat? I thought we would go to the OutBack and get a steak." Zane looked at his son, who was sitting in the backyard in the corner. "Have you ever played any games on Xbox?"

"No, I've never seen one of those. I would hear other kids

talking about playing games, but I didn't know what they were talking about."

"You and I will have dinner, then we'll go to Gamestop and buy an Xbox. We'll both learn how to play."

"Okay."

They were sitting having dinner when Zane felt someone staring at them. Zane dropped his napkin and bent over so he could see behind him. He froze, but the guy looking at him wouldn't know he noticed anything. He saw the man sitting close to the door and knew he had to get Taylor out of there. Anyone looking at them would know they were father and son. *What the hell is he doing out of prison?* "Taylor, you know how I'm an ex-DEA agent, well someone is sitting behind me who is supposed to be locked up in prison right now. He would like nothing better than to see me dead. I want you to get up when I say, and we'll leave together, always stay in front of me. Don't look. I don't want him to know I saw him." Zane picked up his phone and dialed a number. "Lucas, I'm having dinner with my son, and guess who is sitting behind me?"

"Hello Zane, why don't you tell me who is sitting behind you?"

"Thomas Garcia. Isn't he supposed to be locked up? You know he blames me for his brother's death. I don't want anyone to know I have a son. They'll use him against me the first chance they get. Do you think he came to California to find me? I don't want a big fucking shoot-out inside of the restaurant."

"Fuck, can you get out of there without anything happening? You have to make sure he doesn't follow you. I'm going to call a few people and find out what's going on. He is supposed to be locked up. Don't hang up yet. I'll get right back to you."

"Hurry." Zane looked at his son, who looked like he just won the lottery.

"Dad, what are we going to do now?"

"We're going to wait for Lucas to get back on the line. He's married to Skye, and he's Brinley's brother. He's DEA."

"You know a lot of exciting people."

"Yeah, I guess I do. It goes with the business. You'll know all of them soon." His phone beeped, and he put it to his ear.

"The FBI is on their way. If you can get out of there, I would do it now. Maybe he'll walk outside to follow you. I don't want anyone firing their gun into a crowd of people."

"Yeah, we'll leave right now." Zane looked at his son. He held his arm up for the bill. When the waiter brought it over, he took out a hundred and put it on the table. Taylor, I want you to leave first. I'll be two feet behind you."

"Dad, I don't want anything to happen to you."

Nothing is going to happen to me, and nothing is going to happen to you. Just keep walking. Don't look at anyone." Zane made sure his body was blocking Taylor's. He knew when Thomas got up. He knew when he was behind him. Zane heard the click of the gun the instant they were clear of the crowd. He swung his leg around, kicked the gun from Thomas's hand, and had him on the ground before Thomas knew what happened to him.

"Bastard, I'm going to kill your son. You think I don't know who he is. Your son looks just like you. You killed my brother. You will pay for what you did. If it isn't me, then it will be someone else. I already sent his photo out on the internet and offered one million dollars for his death."

Zane knocked the guy out and took his phone. In two minutes, he had changed the order for Thomas's death. He looked up, and his son stood staring at him.

"Can I learn how to do that?"

"I'll start teaching you myself tomorrow." Cars pulled into

the parking lot, and the FBI men walked over to him. "Why the fuck is Thomas Garcia out of prison?"

"He broke out in a delivery truck."

Zane walked closer to the men. "This guy put a hit out on my son. I don't want him going back to prison. I don't give a fuck what you do with him. Get him out of here. He looked over at his son. "Taylor, I think you and I are going to Nashville. I can't wait for Pollyanna to meet you."

"I hope she lets me live in the house."

"Taylor, believe me when I say she will love you. You know no one besides your mom and her boyfriend make children live outside. You will always live inside with us."

"I know. Sometimes I forget."

"I'm going to have you talk to a friend of mine when we get back home. He helped me when my grandfather found me."

"Is it Warren?"

Zane laughed. "No, he is not Warren."

17

Pollyanna was on the children's floor singing to them when Zane walked in. She smiled and looked over at his son. She had a large grin when she saw him. He looked so much like his dad. She loved him already. As soon as the song was finished, she slowly made her way to Zane. He put his arm around her and drew her into his side.

Zane bent his head and kissed her. "I missed you, sweetheart."

"I missed you too. Are you going to introduce me to Taylor?"

Zane looked at Taylor, who looked like he would faint. "Taylor, this is Pollyanna."

"Sugar. Are you Sugar?"

Polly smiled, "Yes, but don't let that get in our way. I'm so happy to meet you, Taylor. We are going to be great friends."

"When you and my dad get married, do I call you Mom?"

"If you want to, of course, you can. I would love for you to call me Mom." Polly wiped a tear from her eye. "I'm sorry to be weepy, but I'm so happy."

They made their way to Polly's room when Taylor looked

over at Polly and shyly spoke. "I'm happy too. Dad said I will always live inside the house with you guys."

Polly thought she would cry. Those bastards who made a baby sleep outside needed to hang from a tree. If she could, she would be the one to do it. Polly took his hand, "You will always sleep inside. Only horrible people would make a child sleep outside. When the baby comes, she'll want her brother with her always."

Zane put his arm around her, "When are they letting you go home?"

"Today, I already have my papers. Since I knew you were coming, I waited for you."

Zane's phone rang. He frowned when he saw who was calling. "What's happened?"

"Thomas Garcia got away," Lucas said. "I still don't have all the information. Two FBI agents are dead. The one who lived is in the hospital in critical condition."

Fuck," he looked at Polly, "I have to take this call. Taylor, you stay here with Pollyanna. Don't go outside. I'll be right back."

"Taylor, we'll wait in my room. You can carry my bag for me." Polly looked at Taylor, "So you listen to country music?"

"I like all music. Your music plays on the pop channel as well as a couple others.

"Yes, it does. Not everyone knows that."

"I was allowed to have a radio, so I learned a lot about music."

"Can you sing?"

"Yes, my music teacher always wanted me to join the choir. I was never allowed to join anything. My teacher wanted to talk to my family, but I couldn't let that happen. Greg would have killed me."

"I'm sorry you went through all of that. I can't even imagine what you went through. I hope Greg and Tracy rot in hell for what they did to you. She started to say something else but looked over and saw Zane standing in the doorway. By the look on his face, she knew something was wrong. She only saw that look when he was angry enough to kill someone.

"What happened?" Polly asked.

"Let's discuss it when we get home." Zane saw Taylor had her bag and stepped out of the room.

"You have to ride in the wheelchair," the nurse said, coming into the room.

"That's okay, I don't mind. I'm a little tired right now." Polly looked at Zane, "As soon as my ribs heal, I'll be fine. You don't have to stay and take care of me. I want you and Taylor to do whatever you want to do. I will be fine. I promise."

"I know you will be, but I love you, and I'm going to help you."

"Okay."

As Zane helped Polly in the vehicle, he bent his head and kissed her. He whispered so only she could hear. "I love you. I'm sorry my life is so busy right now. When we get home, I need to talk to you."

Polly nodded her head in acknowledgment as she sat down. She wondered if Zane had some bad news. She could tell when his expression shut down it wasn't good news. The music playing on the radio relaxed her then she heard Taylor singing in the back seat. His voice made her want to cry. It was pitch-perfect. She looked at Zane, and he looked at her. Both of them knew Taylor could make a good living off his voice. It was beautiful. Polly hummed along with the music.

Zane was ready to kill someone. He couldn't believe that fucking Thomas Garcia was able to escape again. Zane would have to hunt the man down before his henchmen found Taylor and Polly. He regretted making so many enemies in his lifetime. That was his job. He had to take down the cartel and every other drug dealer and human traffickers he could. He never thought he would have a family he had to protect against his enemies. He would take care of them, but first, he had to find Thomas Garcia and kill him. If Taylor hadn't been with him, he would have killed him when he had him. When they pulled into Polly's driveway, she looked back at Taylor. You can pick any room you want, Taylor. There are five bedrooms. So take your pick. I should have stopped at the grocery store and bought more groceries. I'll order some, and they can deliver whatever we need." She took a deep breath. "It sure feels good being out of the hospital. Now, if these bruises will go away, I'll be as good as new."

Zane kissed her when she got out of the vehicle. "I want you to rest, sweetheart. Taylor and I will cook dinner. Isn't that right, Taylor?"

"Yeah, Warren has been teaching me how to cook. We can have a bacon, lettuce and tomato sandwich. Those are really good."

"That sounds great to me," Polly said as she put her arm around his waist. He leaned in but she could tell he wasn't full relaxed. "Do you not want me hugging you?" She didn't want to overstep any boundaries he had. He'd been through enough already.

"No, it's okay. I'm just not used to having anyone touching me."

"Well, I should tell you I'm a hugger and a kisser."

"That's okay. Dad said he was a hugger also."

"That's right, I am," Zane said, ruffling up Taylor's hair. "Why don't you pick a room, and I'll help Pollyanna put her things away."

Okay." He ran upstairs two at a time.

Zane put his arm around Polly, and they walked to her room. As soon as they got inside, he closed the door and gently pulled her to him. "Now, tell me how you really feel, sweetheart?"

"I actually feel pretty good, considering what I went through. Plus, I have this big hunk of a man who loves me. What could be more perfect?"

"Come and sit down, love. I need to talk to you. There is a man who is after Taylor only because he is my son. The bastard broke out of prison. I caught him when Taylor and I ate at a restaurant. The FBI hauled his ass off, but he got away. He knew right away Taylor was my son just by looking at him. He has a hit out on Taylor. So you see why I have to kill him. I have some guys coming here tonight to guard both of you. I'll leave in the morning and track the bastard down. Can you watch over Taylor for me?"

"Of course, I will. I'll guard him with my life. Do you know where to look for this man?"

"Yes, a friend of mine who is undercover saw him, and she called me. Julia said he's hanging out with some others that should be taken down. Julia is Skye's adopted daughter, even though they are only a few years apart. She an FBI special agent also. Skye adopted her and a few others. I'm afraid if I take Taylor, they'll get him."

"Why don't you tell Taylor that you're leaving him here to take care of the baby and me while you go arrest the guy? You don't have to tell him you're going to kill the guy."

Zane chuckled. "Okay, that's what I'll say to him. I hate leaving you. You know that, don't you love?"

"Yes, I know that. I also know I'm going to miss you. I'm happy you're doing this. I know how it feels to be looking over your shoulder all the time for a crazy person to attack you."

18

No one would know the drugged-out guy in the corner was Zane. It's been almost two months since he's been undercover hunting down Thomas Garcia. He hasn't spotted him, even though Julia says he's here in this shit hole of a place where all the fucking scum lived. Someone should take a bulldozer and bring every one of these homemade shacks down. There were more people here than he thought there were. He spotted Julia a few times walking around like she knew what she was doing. He's watched her kicked the crap out of a man last week. Her long brunette hair died a golden blonde, her blue eyes wore green contacts, and she had a dark tan. She was beautiful no matter what color her hair or eyes were. Skye taught her everything she knew about protecting herself, and shewas damn good at it.

He saw someone looking at him and pretended he was spaced out. He talked to himself and shouted at an imaginary person. Then he would start laughing at nothing. He got up and walked to the other end of this hell hole where only drug addicts, dealers, and killers lived, in the desert. He saw a commotion going on and tried to hear what it was about. Then he saw a blonde woman kicking and screaming. *Human trafficking, fuck! What the hell should I do?*

Zane was about to get up when a hand landed on his shoulder. He looked, and Lucas, with a beard and red hair, stood behind him. If Zane hadn't seen his grin, he never would have known who he was. Zane stayed where he was and watched as Julia slammed the guy who held the girl in the face with the palm of her hand. He flew back and landed on his ass. When he reached for his gun, another man pulled his out and shot the guy.

Zane hadn't slept in three days, he must have dozed off because Julia kicked his foot, and he jumped.

"He's gone. Here is the address." Julia pushed a piece of paper under his leg with her dusty boot.

Zane knew he had to get this guy. At least he's been in the hell hole long enough that most of the people there knew he was just a drug addict and didn't pay much attention to what he did. He started singing as he walked away without one person trying to stop him. As soon as he got out of town, he called Julia.

"Thomas is pretty confident that he's never going to be caught. He's bragging about how he can do anything and not get caught. You better be careful. He's got some finger happy jerks on his payroll, and they are looking for Taylor. He has told anyone who would listen to him that it's your fault his brother is dead. He's also hooked on herion so watch yourself."

"Oh yeah, was that one of his men who shot that guy who pulled a gun on you last week?"

"As a matter of fact, it was his guy. Skye said to tell you to hurry and finish this job because Polly is getting big."

Zane chuckled. "I can't wait to see them. You need to be

careful I overheard little Joe say he was going to make you his woman."

"I'll kill that creep if he gets near me. Jake won't let him anywhere around me. I don't know why he is the way he is, but I'm glad he keeps men away from me. I gotta go, Zane. Good luck."

Zane nodded, forgetting she couldn't see him. "I'll see you when this is all over." Zane pictured Pollyanna in his head as being heavy with his child, God he missed her. He missed his son also. It was taking way too long to catch Thomas Garcia. He walked the mile to where his vehicle was parked.

He climbed inside and could smell his body odor. *Damn, no wonder I convinced people I was on drugs. I haven't showered in two weeks.* The first thing he would do is take a shower and shave, and get this dye out of his hair, and put on clean clothes. These ones he would burn. He dialed Pollyanna. It's been two months since he's talked to her. There was no way he would trust calling her while he was in the shit hole he's been in for two months. There was no answer. Then his phone rang.

"Hey Dad, did you get the guy?"

Zane smiled, "Has your voice gotten deeper since I've been gone?"

"Maybe. Polly says I'm bigger than I was so maybe my voice has changed too. When are you coming to get us?"

"I hope it'll be soon. I miss you, Taylor."

"I miss you too, Dad. Polly's taken me fishing, and we went to a major league baseball game. I liked the food they had there. I'm taking care of Polly like you said, Dad."

"Where is she?"

"She's sleeping. The baby made her tired today. Do you want me to wake her?"

Zane did want to wake her, but he knew she needed her

sleep. "No, I'll call back later today. Tell me how you've been?"

"I love being away from where I use to live. Those girls they took were given back to their families. We saw Skye. She said she had to kill Greg. I'm glad she killed him. Tracy is going to prison. The news talked about what happened, and people were angry because I lived in the backyard. Polly wouldn't let anyone know who I was or where I lived. She said that was my past life and not the life I have now. I'm glad she's going to be my mom. I love her, and she loves me too. She's always hugging me. Thank you for finding me, Dad. I sang a song with Polly. It's one of the songs I wrote. We went to the studio and everything. It's going to be on the radio." He spat everything out all at once as if he couldn't wait to tell Zane everything.

"Wow, are you saying I have a famous son?"

"Naw, Dad, I'm just me. I hear Polly. I'll give her the phone. Bye, Dad, I love you."

"Bye, son. I love you too."

"Hello." Zane took a deep breath when he heard her voice.

"Hello, sweetheart. I hear you and Taylor have been staying busy."

"I love him so much, Zane. He is such a great kid. I miss you. Did you kill that bastard?"

"I haven't killed him yet, but I know his address, so it won't be much longer. I can't wait to hold you in my arms, darling."

"There is a lot more of me to hold nowadays. I can't wait to be in your arms. I miss you so much. I've been so worried about you."

"Did Skye explain why I couldn't call you?"

"Yes. Julia called me too," Polly giggled. "She said you stink so bad she didn't like getting around you."

Zane chuckled, "Julia is right. I'll have to take ten showers to get rid of this odor. Hopefully, I'll see you in a week or sooner. I love you, sweetheart."

"I love you too Zane, stay safe for us."

"I will stay safe. Don't worry about me. Bye, darling."

"Bye."

Zane didn't want to lose the sound of Pollyanna's voice. He held the phone to his ear for an extra minute, and closed his eyes. He knew what he had to do to keep his family safe. He took a deep breath and started the truck.

19

"Why don't you let us check it out first?"

"Because this is my fight. I should have killed Thomas when I had him. If Taylor hadn't been with me, I would have. Now I have to make sure he dies."

"This isn't just your fight. This is everyone's fight. Thomas Garcia is nothing but shit. He's a danger to every human on this earth. He should have died years ago. Can I come with you and make sure he's killed."

Zane looked over at Storm, "Alright, but don't get in my way." He shook his head, "I swear you are more stubborn than any person I know. Why are you not with the others at my place guarding Willow and Ruby?"

"It's my two weeks off, and I have nothing else to do."

"Have you ever heard of relaxing, Storm? Lounge by the pool with a cold beer. Invite your woman over and play spin the bottle. Do something fun."

"I don't have a woman."

"Well, who the hell's fault is that? Didn't you get yourself shipped off to New York? Did I tell you I spoke to Frankie? She's the one who sent Jason Burks to Pollyanna."

Storm hid his expression and didn't want to say anything. Zane wouldn't turn his head until Storm said something. "Okay, how is she?"

"I spoke to her on the phone, I didn't see her, but she sounded like she was doing great. I asked her if she wanted me to say anything to anyone. Frankie said nope, he's the one who left."

"What the fuck was I supposed to do. Hell, every other day, she had me trading places with Austin. Then she wanted me to come back. I felt like a damn yoyo."

"That's because you two were so hot for each other. You should have just done the deed and got it out of your system."

"If I did the deed with Frankie, it would never get out of my system. She is a classy woman. I was her bodyguard. We did have hot electricity jumping from us, but I couldn't take advantage of her. She couldn't get around with a broken leg, and she was stuck there on her uncle's ranch."

"She is a grown woman. Maybe Frankie wanted you to take advantage of her. If you're going to be stuck somewhere, what better place is there to be than on a horse ranch."

"Can we not talk about Dr Frankie Strong, please?"

"Let's go and get this ass hole."

"I'm ready. How's Polly doing?"

"Taylor said she's getting big. She has six weeks before the baby is due. I want to be with them. Julia said this guy has been hunting for me. I have to stop him before he finds my family. Do you want to stop and get something to eat?"

"Yeah, I'll take a cheeseburger."

"Do you ever want to stop and eat a real sit-down meal?"

"No, I'm too impatient for that. I like eating on the go."

Zane shook his head and chuckled. He pulled into Carl Juniors where they grilled there burgers, and ordered four bacon avocado cheeseburgers with fries and two large drinks. He knew Storm could eat three of those cheeseburgers. He's seen him do it. While they ate their food, he looked up the address where Thomas was staying. "Look at this. He's around the corner from here."

Storm put the remains of their lunch in a bag and walked it to the garbage. He looked at the vehicle they were using. It had dark windows so no one could see who was inside. He opened the door, got in, and shut it. "I think you should look at who's standing over there. Is that the guy you're looking for?"

Zane looked and couldn't believe his luck. The bastard stood fifteen feet from him. Zane looked around and noticed other people sitting at the tables outside. He couldn't shoot him with all these people around here. But he could walk up and arrest him. Sure he's no longer a DEA agent, but sometimes he does jobs for them. He looked over at Storm, "I'm going to arrest him."

"What if he starts shooting when he sees you? I think it would be better if you let me go in and arrest him. I've been a homicide detective for years, plus he doesn't know me."

"How do you know he doesn't know who you are?"

"I've never had reason to be in his company before. He won't know who I am. I'll walk up and have him down before he knows what hit him."

"Damn it. You're right. Let's do this." Zane got out on his side, and Storm got out on his side. He didn't hesitate a second. He walked up to Thomas and that's when he heard the gunshots. He pulled his gun out. He didn't look to see who fired the weapon his was pointed at Thomas Garcia, and Storm didn't have time to think about what he was going to do. The point of Thomas's gun was aimed at him. He rolled across the pavement and shot Thomas. He didn't have to check to see if the guy was dead. He made sure if he was aiming his gun, it was to kill. He ran around the side of the vehicle and saw two dead men. He turned and saw Zane on the ground in a pool of blood. "Call nine-one-one," he shouted to the people who were gathering. "Is there a doctor around here? I need some help. Agent Taylor has been shot." Storm thought if he said agent, they would be more likely to help. He felt Zane for a pulse and could find nothing. "Zane, open your damn eyes." He ripped Zane's shirt open and saw two spots where the bullets went.

"Let me see him. I'm a nurse," a woman said, tugging Storm out of the way. She pushed on Zane's chest, trying to get his heart beating. She wouldn't stop.

Storm watched as she kept it up. Storm knew the instant Zane's heart started beating again. Then he saw the blue around Zane's lips leaving. "You did it. You saved his life."

"No, I only kept him alive for when the ambulance gets here. Hopefully, they'll be able to keep him alive. Let me check his wounds. That was some crazy stuff. Who were those guys?"

"They escaped from prison. I don't know how they recognized us. Unless they saw Zane pull into the drive-through window."

"Good, here comes the ambulance. I got to go. I hope he makes it."

"Wait, what's your name?"

"Nancy Winters. I'll pray for your friend."

"Thank you, Nancy. You saved Zane's life."

Zane was rushed to the hospital. Storm followed behind the ambulance. He called Killian and told him everything that happened. "It was like they were waiting for us. I don't know how they knew who I was. I'm the only one who got out of the car. As soon as I walked ten feet or so from the truck, the bullets must have shot Zane. He managed to kill two men, and I killed Thomas Garcia. Who's going to call Polly?"

"Let's wait and see how Zane is before we call her. When

is the baby due?"

"Zane said in six weeks."

"Hmm, I don't know how she's going to react. I don't want her to go into labor. Why don't I call Rowan and he can tell Missy. She'll probably fly to Tennessee to be with Polly."

"That's a good idea. I'll let you know how Zane is as soon as the doctor tells me something."

"Okay, I'll be there as soon as I can get there."

Storm waited five hours part of that time with his buddies in and out. He was there with Marc and Jonah when the doctor walked into the waiting room. All of them stood up.

"Are you all with Zane Taylor?"

"Yep," Storm said, waiting to hear what he had to say.

"It was touch and go. He died twice on the table before we were able to stabilize him. We are going to have to wait and see how it goes in the next twenty-four to forty-eight hours." He heard a noise behind him and turned around. Polly, Missy, and Taylor stood in the doorway.

Storm walked to where she stood. "What are you doing here? I thought Missy would be with you in Tennessee. How's the baby?"

Polly shook her head, then she took a deep breath and turned to talk to the doctor. "I want to see my husband right now." She glared at the guys daring them to say anything.

"When they take him to ICU, you can see him. As I was telling these men, your husband was fortunate. But he still has a fight on his hands. You being here may be just what he needs. I'll send a nurse in when you can visit."

"Thank you, doctor." Polly still had a hold of Taylor's hand. "His son and I both will visit him."

The doctor nodded once. He recognized Sugar right away and was a little awe-struck with her. He thought she was more beautiful up close, than on TV.

Polly put her arm around Taylor. "He's going to be okay. Let's sit down until the nurse comes." She looked at the men sitting across from her. "Who wants to tell us what happened?"

"Maybe I should take Taylor for a walk or something," Missy offered.

"No, it's okay. I don't want to keep anything from him. He's worried about his dad just as much as we are."

Storm spoke up, "Okay. We were at Carls Junior eating. When I took the bag to the garbage, I noticed Thomas Garcia sitting on a bench. I told Zane, and we agreed he didn't know me, so I would confront him. It was a set-up. I don't know how they knew we were there. I had only taken a few steps when I heard the gunfire. I shot Thomas, who had his gun pointed at me. When I ran around the truck, I saw Zane on the ground and two other men dead. Zane wasn't breathing. I shouted for someone to call nine-one-one and asked if there was a medic who could help. A nurse ran over and got his heart beating and stayed with us until the ambulance got there."

"Did you get her name?"

"Yes, it's Nancy Winters."

"She saved his life. If Nancy hadn't been there, Zane would be gone now." Polly wiped her eyes. "Do all of you know my son, Taylor?"

"Yeah, how you doing, Taylor? Were you surprised to find out Polly was Sugar?" Storm said with a chuckle trying to get him to focus on something other than his father.

"Yeah, I'm going to have the coolest mom at school."

They all laughed. "Why don't you stay at the safe house while you're here?"

"We're going to stay with Missy. Thank you for asking. Missy wants Taylor to hang out with her. This is her first cousin."

The nurse walked in and looked around. She was a little flustered seeing all these gorgeous men in this small waiting area. Her eyes darted around until they landed on Polly. "Oh my God, Sugar, I love you."

"Thank you, did you come about Zane Taylor?"

"Yes, are you his wife?"

"Yes," again she looked at the men daring them to say anything.

"You can follow me. I'll take you to your husband."

Polly looked at Taylor, "Do you want me to go first?"

"Is it okay if I wait until you see him first?"

"Of course it is, sweetheart." Polly followed the nurse, "How would I find a nurse by the name of Nancy Winters? Do you know if she works here? I know there are hundreds of nurses here, but Nancy saved Zane's life."

"You can go to the emergency room, Nancy Winters works there. I went to school with her."

"She got his heart to start beating, and she got him to breathe again. Without her, Zane wouldn't be here with us right now."

"Yep, that's Nancy. She's a beautiful human being."

"I agree." Polly took a deep breath before walking into the cubicle where Zane laid with wires everywhere. She looked at him, and the tears flowed. He looked so helpless with all the tubes and wires everywhere. She sat down in the chair because the baby was kicking up a storm. The baby must have known something was wrong. The nurse left them alone. "Hey sweetheart, I'm here. Taylor is here also. We love you; please fight with everything you got to come back to us. I know it's hard, but remember, we are here for you. We are spending the rest of our lives together. This precious baby inside of me needs her daddy, and you have a son in the waiting room who loves you and needs you so much." She sniffled.

"I'm going to stay right here beside you until you wake up. I'm sorry I put you through what I'm going through. Why don't both of us stop working where we have crazy people wanting to harm us? I want to spend every day with you and our children," she added.

"Taylor and I recorded a song together. He wrote it. I couldn't have stopped myself from singing that song with him. It is the most beautiful moving song I have ever heard. We'll sing it for you. I hope you don't get angry, but I had Jonah put some papers together saying Taylor is my son. I didn't want anything to happen to him in case something terrible happened to you. We don't have to worry about that anymore. I'm going to go get your son so he can see you're going to be okay," she continued.

Polly walked back to the waiting area, she looked around at the people in the waiting room. All of these people cared for Zane. "I believe Zane is going to be okay. He's a little pale, and there are lots of wires and tubes on him, but I'm sure when he wakes up, he'll be fine, and want all those wires off. Taylor, are you ready to see your dad?"

"Yes, will he wake up soon?"

"He'll wake up when his body says he can. Right now, it's healing, so it might take a few days. I told him we would sing your song to him. Don't worry about how he looks. Those wires and tubes are doing a job, and he needs them." She held onto Taylor's hand as they walked to where Zane was as much for her as for Taylor.

Taylor stopped at the end of the bed and stared at his Dad, "My Dad was the first person in the world to love me. You were the second, and Missy said she loves me too. I don't want to go back to that other life. I love all of you."

Polly put her arm around him, "You will never go back to anything. You are mine and Zane's son, and you will always be our son. I will never let anyone take you from us."

Taylor wiped his eyes. "Dad, please wake up."

"Sit down, sweetheart. I'll get another chair."

"You sit down. I'll get the chair." Taylor looked at Polly. "How is the baby? The guys were afraid you would go into labor."

Polly chuckled, "Let me tell you something, honey. Women are way stronger than men, not in strength but in everything else. There is nothing wrong with that. Women can handle stress way better than men. I'm fine, and the baby is fine. We still have some weeks before she will be here. Wow, I just remembered all of the baby's things are in Tennessee. What are we going to do? We'll have to go shopping." Polly frowned, thinking. "I'll order everything online. It should be here in plenty of time. We'll stay with Missy until Zane's home is ready for us to move into. I'll order the clothes, and you can order the baby bed and changing table. Be sure to get the rocking chair. You can have Missy help you pick it out. I'm going to stay at the hospital with Zane. If you want to go home with Missy, you can. Let me give you a credit card so you can order the baby furniture."

"I have a credit card. Dad gave it to me."

"He did. I swear your dad thinks of everything." Polly looked at Zane, then she looked at Taylor. They looked so much alike, and since Taylor has put on weight and muscle, he really looked like him. When he grinned at her, her heart melted. "Do you want me to walk back to the waiting room with you?"

"No, I'm okay. I'll stay here with you if you want me to."

"I'll be fine. You can come back later if you want. I'm going to stay the night here. That way, when Zane wakes up, he'll see me."

"Will you call me if I'm not here when he wakes up?"

"You'll be the first one I call." She smiled at her son.

20

*P*olly's back killed her, Nancy who was now her friend, looked at her as they ate lunch in the hospital cafeteria. "You should go home and get some rest. You need to save your strength for when the baby arrives."

"I'll be fine as soon as Zane wakes up. It's been six days. I'm scared, and so is Taylor. I don't know what to tell him anymore."

"Tell him the truth. Zane will wake up when his body wants to wake up. He's healing right now. He'll wake up soon, I promise you."

"How can you promise me that he'll wake up?"

"Because I feel it." Nancy burst into laughter at the look on Polly's face. "You should see your face. It is so funny."

Polly chuckled, "I need to get back to Zane. I'm glad he has a private room now." She stopped and looked at Nancy. "Do you feel he'll wake up today?"

"Today or tomorrow."

Polly shook her head and walked away. She felt as if she's known Nancy forever. Nancy has three children, ages sixteen, fourteen, and ten. Her husband ran off with his secretary six years ago. Her children don't want anything to do with him. Nancy told her he called six months after he ran out on them begging to come back. She said she laughed and hung up the phone on him. Nancy said a few months after he left, the family noticed how much stress had left their house. There was no way in hell she wanted him back. She doesn't know it, but Polly bought her a house and completely furnished it. Piper is taking care of all that for her. She's going to tell Nancy she entered her in a lottery or something. She was still working on all of that stuff. When her husband left, she couldn't keep up the payments and rented a smaller home. Polly owed her so much more. But Nancy refused to accept anything from Polly, so she had no choice but to be sneaky. She tried to get comfortable later that night when Nancy walked into Zane's room.

"Are you in pain?"

"It's my back. It still hurts. Why are you still here?"

"I did an extra shift." She looked at how Polly stood, it looked like the baby had dropped. "Polly, are you in labor?"

"No, I have a few weeks to go."

"Are you sure?"

"I think I do. I'm pretty sure. I don't know I may have got the dates wrong."

"Come with me. We're going to the sixth floor to have you checked out."

"No, Zane needs to be with me when the baby comes. I'm not leaving this room."

Nancy got on the phone and ordered a delivery bed, then she called the labor floor and asked if they could send a doctor to Zane's room.

Polly tried to get her to stop. She wasn't in labor. Her back hurt from sitting so long. "I'll walk around. That'll take the pain away."

"After you are examined, I'll walk with you. Walking is good if you are in labor."

"I'm not in labor."

"Better safe than sorry."

∽

Zane could hear them talking. He tried to force his eyes open. But he couldn't open them. He tried to move his hand so he could touch Polly, but he didn't know if his fingers moved or not. He didn't want Pollyanna to go through this on her own. *Damn it, eyes, please open for me. Why won't they open?*

"This isn't necessary," Polly said as she put the gown on behind the curtain. She glanced at Zane. She thought he moved his hand. Polly put her hand in his and kissed him. "Open your eyes, sweetheart. It's time for our baby to be born. I've held them off as long as I could."

Zane opened his eyes. He looked at Polly, but he still couldn't talk. He saw tears fall from her eyes. Polly took his hand and put it on her tummy. He moved his fingers. "Stay awake until our daughter arrives, okay."

Zane nodded once before his eyes started to close.

"Nancy, can you please call Taylor and let him and Missy know the baby will be here real soon."

Nancy pulled the curtain away and frowned, "So, you have been in labor."

"I wasn't sure, but my water just broke. Zane opened his eyes. He promised to stay awake. But I think he went back to sleep."

Zane shook his head, "I'm awake, love," he said almost inaudibly.

Polly burst into tears and got on the bed. "I love you, Zane."

"I love you, sweet." The nurse called Zane's doctor.

～

Polly's delivery bed was set up in Zane's room, only because she refused to leave his room. Polly didn't want Zane to miss anything. She didn't want to cry out from the labor pain. She didn't want to upset Zane, but she couldn't stop the sound of pain that came from her as the baby arrived.

"Polly, sweetheart."

"Zane, it's okay. Our baby is here." The doctor laid the baby on Polly's chest. She looked down at her brand new baby. Tears spilled from her eyes. She looked over at Zane, then at Nancy. "Here, Nancy let Zane give his daughter a kiss."

"Polly, umm, you should look at the baby," Nancy said, grinning.

Polly raised her baby up and smiled. "I wanted a boy. He's the image of his daddy. She looked at Zane. I'll have to buy more baby clothes. Nancy, please take him to his daddy before Zane falls asleep."

Zane closed his eyes as the nurse held his son up to him. He kissed his son. He wanted to hold him, but he still couldn't raise his hands. "I love you, baby. Pollyanna, we have to name him."

"We will. We'll let Taylor help us."

Zane thought of his son, Taylor, and felt like he wanted to break down and cry at how he was treated. He looked at Polly and knew she was thinking the same thing. "I've missed you, sweetheart."

"I've missed you so much, Zane."

"Okay, folks, we have to call everyone to order. Polly, you are going to the delivery floor, and I need to check out Zane."

"My Dad's awake," Taylor said, rushing into the room. He

walked over to his dad and hugged him. "Dad, I was so scared you wouldn't wake up."

"I just needed a little rest. I won't stay away from you that long ever again. You have grown so much. I missed you, son. From now on, our family will always be together. Are you going to say hello to the baby?"

"What baby?" His eyes were as big as saucers when he looked at Polly. "My sister is here?"

Polly smiled and shook her head, "No, your baby brother is here. Come and meet him."

Taylor walked over and touched the baby's face. His eyes teared up. "I thought I was getting a sister."

"So did we," Zane said.

Taylor looked down at his little brother. "I swear to both of you, I won't let anything bad happen to my brother. What's his name?"

"You'll have to help us with that," Polly said.

"Are you happy he's not a she?"

"Yes, sweetheart, I don't care what our baby is as long as he's healthy. Now I'm so proud I have two boys who I love so much. Give me a hug, sweetheart. I love you with all my heart. I want you to always remember that."

Taylor was getting used to Polly telling him how much she loved him, but he still blushed. He loved her so much he decided he would make her happy. "I know Mom, I love you too."

Polly took hold of his cheeks, "That's right, I'm your mom for always."

He nodded because he didn't want to embarrass himself by crying in front of Missy.

"I hate to break all this up, but we need to do things," Nancy said as she wiped her eyes dry. "Your mom has to go to the delivery floor. You can stay here for a while with your dad until Missy comes and gets you."

Taylor stood up straight, "Okay, nurse Nancy, thank you." He watched as they wheeled his mom and new baby brother out of the room. He looked at his dad, "Thank you, Dad, for finding me."

"I think we should call Jason Burks up and thank him. Maybe we'll take him fishing with us one day. Can you come and sit with me while I sleep?"

"Okay. That nurse with mom is Nancy. She saved your life when you were shot."

"You'll have to move your chair. We need to get in here and see how your dad is doing."

Taylor picked up his chair and smiled as he moved it to the other side. He saw his dad look at Nancy as she walked behind the bed, following his mom.

21

Polly smiled at Missy and Nancy as she put on her lipgloss. "I'm so excited. I'll be Zane's wife in just a little bit. Taylor walks me down the aisle, and then he'll walk over to Zane's side and be his best man. The entire time Zane will be holding the baby, and Missy will be my maid of honor. My whole family will be involved in my wedding."

"I'm so happy for you."

"Have you checked to see if you won anything on those raffle tickets I gave you?"

"I forgot all about my tickets. I'll check on it tomorrow. Did you win anything with yours?"

"No, but I heard no one has won the main prize. Maybe you won the grand prize, and you don't even know it."

"Yeah, that would be awesome. I've never won anything. Maybe my luck has changed since meeting all of you."

Polly smiled. She would let Sage know Nancy was going to call.

"Mom, are you ready?" Taylor called, knocking on the door.

Polly opened the door, "Yes, I'm ready. Let's do this,

Taylor." She smiled when Missy rushed past her to get where she was supposed to be. "Today, we'll become a complete family. I will have the same last name as my children and Zane." A tear slipped out, and Polly wiped it off. She promised herself she wouldn't cry today. They walked down the aisle in the cute little church on the way to Rowan and Piper's house. Most of their friends were there, except the ones guarding Willow and the baby. When she got to Zane, he kissed her.

"Are you ready to become my wife?"

"Yes, this is the best day of my life. I have my family and friends sharing this beautiful moment with us."

"Are we ready?" the pastor said, clearing his throat.

Both Zane and Polly said yes. The sun shined through the stained glass windows. Zane felt like his grandfather watched the whole wedding and knew Zane made the right decision. No one could ever love a woman like he loved Pollyanna. He knew they would have a wonderful life together.

∽

"POLLYANNA, no, you are not going. We've been married for two months. Carter is too young to leave him. We agreed you would take two years off touring."

"It's not a tour, Zane. It's a benefit concert for charity. Why would you think I would leave my baby? All of you are going with me. It's for one weekend only. You know how much the farmers lost during the big freeze they had this winter. They have no money to even buy fuel for their tractors. One hundred percent of the money goes to the farmers. Shay arranged this concert, and I volunteered to sing. I also want Taylor to sing with me. That way, he will come out of his shell and mingle with other singers."

"Only if I can stand on stage with you."

"If I sing you the song I wrote about you, will you dance with me?"

"Baby, nothing could stop me from dancing with you. I love you so much. How big of a benefit is this?"

"Have you heard of Woodstock? It'll probably match that concert."

"Damn, let's take your bus that way the baby will have a place to sleep, and you can feed him in private. Do you think Missy would want to go? We'll see if Warren wants to come along. He can drive the bus."

"I've already asked Missy, she said she would love to go, and Warren has already started packing."

Zane laughed out loud and pulled Polly into his arms. "Let's go upstairs and take a nap, sweetheart," Zane said, bending his head and kissing Polly.

Polly laughed as she ran upstairs with Zane on her heels. The baby was sleeping, and Taylor was in the pool with Missy. They were still at Missy's because they hadn't caught Willow's ex-father-in-law yet.

Polly lay in Zane's arms after they made passionate love with each other. "Zane, are you going to go back to work?" Polly asked with a frown on her face.

"I don't know if I am. If I do, it won't be for a couple of years. I'm busy with Taylor, and I enjoy being home with you and Carter."

"Good, I like being with you too. How would we ever go back to work full time and leave our children? I never want to leave them or you. I love the way our family is right now. I don't want to change anything."

"I don't want to change anything either. Pollyanna, I'm having the best time I've ever had in my life. I've never felt this content before. I never knew loving you could bring me so much joy."

"I know, that's exactly how I feel," Polly said, kissing him.

Zane pulled her under him. He was ready for more passionate sex with his beautiful wife. Then they heard the baby. "I'll get him and bring him to you," Zane said, getting out of bed.

Polly watched him walk over to the crib naked as the day he was born. He picked his baby up and kissed him. It surprised her and all of their friends how much Zane has changed. He laughed more, and he loved more. He was always hugging Taylor, telling him how much he loved him. The old Zane walked around frowning. The new Zane smiled all the time.

22

Polly looked around the area where the busses were. Theirs was parked next to Shay's bus. Killian and Bird were there as well. They had baby's running around in the area that was fenced off, while Zane laughed at Killian, who tried catching Gracie. Killian scooped her up and threw her in the air while she screamed for more. Marc's sister Maddy was there to help them, but she wanted to see one of her favorite singers.

Zane carried Carter and Killian put his kids in a three-person walker. All the children had ear muffs on because the music was so loud. As they walked up to where the music was, Pollyanna and Taylor were getting ready to sing. Zane saw his wife squeeze Taylor's hand. Then they began to sing. Pollyanna went first, the crowd was so quiet they knew the story of Polly and her handsome son. It was in the papers after Zane took him home. They loved Taylor and Polly.

They sang their number one hit. It's been in the top one hundred for weeks. The crowd went wild. Then Taylor surprised all of them by saying he had a song he wanted to sing. Zane could tell Polly was surprised. She nodded her head and walked to the back of the stage as Taylor sang his song. The girls were screaming. They loved him when he finished. There was a loud roar as the crowd shouted out as one. TAYLOR. Zane was so proud of him he stepped up on stage with his baby in his arms and put his arms around his son.

"Did you write me that song? I love it." He didn't realize everyone was listening to him over the speakers. No one said a word. They wanted to hear what Zane told his son. "The day I found you was the day my life changed forever. I never knew a parent could love their child so much. You bring so much to my life, son. I love you."

"I love you too, Dad."

Everyone in the audience had tears in their eyes, and the girls were screaming they loved Taylor, while women were screaming for Zane. That's when he realized he was on speaker. He actually blushed as he put his other arm around his son, and they walked to where Polly stood. She put her sunglasses on so the people couldn't see her crying. She hugged Taylor, then she took the baby from Zane.

"I need to feed him. I think I'll go back to the bus for now."

Zane put his arm around her when she sniffed. She didn't fool him or Taylor, they knew she was crying. "I'll go with you. Here comes Missy and Maddy."

"Hey Taylor, want to hang out with us for a while?"

Taylor looked at his dad. "Go ahead, have fun. Don't let yourself get separated from each other. I know I sound paranoid, but hey, I know how the world works. I want all of you to be safe."

"Okay, Dad," all three of them said at the same time. They looked at each other and laughed.

Zane walked back to the bus with his arm around

Pollyanna, "Do you want to take a nap?" Zane asked, smiling at Pollyanna.

Polly laughed, "No, people will be stopping by all day to say hello. I'm sorry, darling, but we'll have to wait until we get home. There is no way I'm going to do anything in the bus." Polly laughed. "We'd have to put up a sign that said: If This Bus Is Rocking Don't Bother Knocking."

"Hey, that's fine with me. I'll go find a sign right now."

"What will you tell Taylor when he asks about the rocking bus?" She burst out laughing.

"Okay, we'll wait until we get home, but it's going to be damn hard keeping my hands off of you."

Polly was right. Someone stopped by every time Zane turned around. He met some very famous people who wanted to congratulate them on their wedding and the baby. Most of all, they wanted to say how happy they were about him finding Taylor. It was getting dark when Taylor made his way back to the bus with Missy. They had already walked Maddy to where Killian and Bird parked their bus.

"Did you have a nice time?" Polly asked him as she handed him a plate of food Warren passed to her.

"Yes, I'm having a great time. After I eat, can I hold the baby for a while? I miss him. When we are home, I could pick him up anytime, but I've been busy here. I don't want him to think his big brother doesn't love him."

"Taylor, he would never think that. How could he ever think that? You tell him every time you see him."

"That's because I never knew what love meant until Dad found me. It's such a heartfelt feeling I want to share it."

Polly and Zane smiled at each other. "It is a beautiful feeling. I agree with you. I'm singing early tomorrow at ten. We'll head over to Nashville and pick up some of my things. I left in such a hurry I didn't get to take the things I want to keep with me. Items that belonged to my mom and grandma, I want to pass down to my daughter."

Maybe the next baby will be a girl. If not, you can try again. I want lots of brothers and sisters."

Zane laughed out loud. "You might have to wait until you are married to have lots of them. Polly and I discussed this already we are having four kids. I think that's a good number."

"That gives you two more tries. Mom, I'll bet the next one is a girl."

"We shall see next year. I want to have children while I can still run after them. I don't know about you two, but I'm going to bed. Zane, will you put the baby to bed after his brother holds him."

"Yes, sweetheart, I'll put him to bed when I go to bed."

Polly put the pillow over her head so Taylor or their neighbors couldn't hear her. Zane came to bed and decided to pleasure his wife and he was doing a great job of it. He started by kissing her navel and went down from there. When his tongue touched her, she almost moaned out loud until she put the pillow over her face. Between Zane's tongue and his fingers, Polly had four orgasms. When Zane made his way back up to her, she decided to pleasure her husband. She threw the pillow over his face and took him into her mouth. They made love in so many different ways that night. It wasn't until the middle of the night they went to sleep.

"Hey, sweetheart, are you going to stay in bed all day?"

Polly sat up and looked at the clock. "Why didn't you wake me earlier? I have to sing at ten."

"I knew how tired you were, but Carter has been trying to drink everyone's milk that held him."

Polly giggled, "Let me see him. Hey, there, my little lovey, are you hungry?" He grabbed hold of a nipple-like he was starving. Polly smiled when Zane laughed out loud.

"He's just like his dad," Zane said, smiling at the way his son sucked on Pollyanna's breast.

∼

ZANE WATCHED the people as Pollyanna sang to them. He stood in the back of the stage so he could keep his eyes on his wife. *There are too many men here who loved her,* is what he thought. Zane wasn't about to share her with anyone. She looked back at him while she sang the song she wrote for him, then she walked around and took his hand. Polly pulled him to where he was visible to the crowd. Damn, she looked sexy. Polly watched his mouth until he bent his head and kissed her. She kept on singing. When the song was over, Zane pulled her to him and kissed her deeply. "I love you, Pollyanna Taylor."

"I love you, Zane Taylor. Now let's go home."

They had just left Polly's house when they got the call. There was a shooting at Zane's home, and Storm was pronounced dead at the hospital. Zane listened as Ash told him what happened. "I got into a fight with one of the security guards there. Poor guy didn't even know how to fight. One punch, and he was down. They called the cops, and we were arrested. We're still in jail. You are my one call. I need you to call Jonah and have him get us out of here. I need to get back to the hospital. Frankie was in the emergency room when we got there. She was trying to bring Storm back to life. I don't know. She may have been arrested too. She was telling all of them in a booming voice to fuck off. The head of the hospital was there. He kept telling Frankie to stop trying to save Storm he was dead. You don't want to know what she told him."

"My God, is he dead?"

"I don't know. That's why I need to get the hell out of

here. I have to get back to the hospital. Call Jonah. He'll know what to do."

"How did they get past my security?"

"They came in a giant Hummer with a bulldozer on the front of it. They bulldozed their way in there. They took out your wall. Willow's ex-father-in-law is dead. Storm killed him and the others that were with him."

"What about Willow and the baby?"

"They're safe."

"I'll call Jonah right now." Zane looked over at Pollyanna. Shaking his head. He couldn't believe Storm was dead. "They killed Storm."

"What? Who killed Storm?"

"Willow's father-in-law."

"Maybe it's a mistake."

"Ash was at the hospital when he was pronounced dead. Now he's in jail. I have to call Jonah to get them out."

"Zane, you were pronounced dead twice. Maybe he's alive. Call and talk to the others."

THE END

BOOKS BY SUSIE MCIVER

https://www.amazon.com/~/e/B079VDSNRM

If you enjoyed Zane's story, can you please leave me a review. Amazon shows our books by how many reviews it gets.

You're going to love Storm's story. Keep reading to see what happens with Storm.

23

STORM
CHAPTER 1

"How the fuck did they find her?" Storm shouted as he ran toward the vehicle. He saw the hummer with the steel guard on the front of it. It looked like a damn bulldozer as it plowed through the thick steel gates at Zane's place. Storm knew this was bad. He ran, shouting for someone in the house to hear him at the same time all the alarms went off all over the property. Marc opened the back door while Storm aimed his gun at the son of a bitch who smiled at him. Storm fired and got to see the shock on the man's face before bullets riddled his own body. The pressure of the bullets lifted him off the ground and threw his body thirty feet backward.

Ash shouted when he saw his buddy fly in the air by the impact of the bullets hitting his body. Gino lay dead. The same man who wanted his ex-daughter-in-law murdered so he could take her baby. How the hell did they find her?

The guys in the hummer were all dead before they knew what happened to them. Ash and Austin killed all four of them. They put Storm in their vehicle and rushed him to the hospital. Marc and Rhys would take Willow and the baby to the safe house.

Willow spat on the dead man and kicked him. "I hope you burn in hell, you bastard. She shouted. She would have kicked him again if Rhys hadn't picked her up and put her in the vehicle."

"Willow, stop screaming at him. He's dead and can't hear you. Kane and Killian are calling the authorities. I want you and Ruby out of here before they show up," Rhys said, looking at her until she calmed down.

"He is a stupid bastard! He had his son killed because he wanted out of the mob."

"I know he is. Now buckle your seatbelt. Gino will burn in hell."

Marc handed the baby to her as she buckled up. She would have kicked the bastard harder if Rhys hadn't made her get in the car. "I'm sorry, but I'm glad he's dead. They wouldn't have kept him locked up. He knows too many people."

Marc, couldn't concentrate. All he could think of was Storm flying backward in the air as the bullets hit his body. "I agree. You don't have to tell me."

"Where did Ash, Austin, and Storm go?"

"They went to the hospital. Storm was shot."

"What! How bad was it?"

"I don't know if he lived."

"What, oh my God, this is my fault."

"He killed your ex-father-in-law before they got him."

"Let's go to the hospital. I want to see how Storm is."

Rhys shook his head, "Are you crazy? We don't know if there are more people out there wanting to kill you. We can't do anything foolish."

"Do you think there are more people? And no, I am not

crazy. All though I should be by now being around you guys all the time."

Marc looked in the rearview mirror. "We don't know if there are more people out there waiting to kill you. That's why we are not taking any chances."

∽

THE HOSPITAL GUARD actually thought they could tell Ash and Austin to leave the emergency room when some stupid doctor pronounced Storm dead.

"Can someone with some fucking brains do something? Make Storm's heart start beating again. I know he still has a chance."

∽

FRANKIE STRONG KNEW THAT VOICE. She ran over and looked at who was on the gurney. "Storm no," she whispered in an anguished voice. "Cut these clothes away and find the holes in his body." Frankie didn't know she was crying. She was not going to let Storm die. She loved this man. *I should have told him. Why didn't I just tell him I loved him?*

"Doctor Strong, he's dead. Stop what you are doing."

"Fuck you!" Frankie growled, not caring who heard her. She never did like Doctor Hinkle; it felt good to tell him that. "Fuck you!" She shouted again.

He looked like he wanted to throw a punch her way. Frankie didn't know any of this because she never raised her head. Ash and Austin noticed that's why they stepped up to where Frankie worked on Storm, shouting orders at everyone in the emergency room. She worked for thirty minutes before the monitor made a beautiful noise. She knew he still had a heart that beat. It just was hard to detect.

"Let me finish for you, Doctor Strong."

"No, I'll do all of it. Don't touch him. Nurse Joy, can you please call and get me an operating room."

"I've already taken care of that Doctor."

"Thank you. The sooner, the better." Frankie was probing the holes she could see. Some of the bullets were still in there. From the corner of her eye, she saw the security guard fall to the floor. Ash had knocked him out. She heard Storm moan in pain. "I'm sorry, Storm. I'm sorry." A nurse handed Frankie a clean towel to wipe the tears away, but Frankie didn't know she was crying. The nurses, who were her friends, had to wipe their tears away themselves. Frankie wouldn't take her eyes from Storm. His black as coal hair fell on his forehead, and she moved it back.

Ash walked over and took Storm's hand so he could squeeze it if he was in pain.

"How the hell did this happen?" Frankie cried. She glanced at Ash. "Get a mask for this man."

"A nurse handed a mask to Ash. Then went back to work helping Frankie.

"I have an operating room for you, doctor. "

"Let's go," Frankie looked at Ash and Austin. "You'll have to wait in the waiting room. You can go to the waiting room on the fourth floor."

Dr. Hinkle walked up to Frankie, "I'll take it from here, Dr. Strong."

Frankie looked at him like he had lost his mind. "Dr. Hinkle, you sure as hell won't take over. I am the only one who is operating on Storm. You need to get the hell out of my way."

Another Security guard walked up to her. "I'm relieving you of your duties. I want you out of my hospital." Dr. Hinkle said, motioning for the security guard to remove her.

"I'll get out after I operate on Storm. This is not your

hospital. Get the hell out of my way." She pushed the bed with the help of the orderly. Completely ignoring Dr. Hinkle. She never did like that man. Frankie looked at Ash and Austin as the police arrested them. "How did the police get here so fast?"

Joy whispered so only she could hear. "He has a policeman here to arrest you too. He called them when you started working on this man."

"When they take me away, call my Uncles. But I'll be damn if I let anyone else operate on Storm." She looked at the security guard, and he stepped away.

She made it to the operating room without being arrested. She looked at Joy. I want you to call Dr. Burks and tell him everything. I want him here taking over for me when they arrest me." The nurses had everything ready for Frankie. The anesthesiologist was there. He gave Storm a shot so he wouldn't wake up during surgery. Frankie and the nurses cut all of Storm's clothes from him except his boxers. He was all muscle. Frankie already knew how strong he was. He carried her around when she broke her leg, hunting for her mom in the mountains. Storm picked her up like she was a feather. She fell madly in love with him the first time she saw him on that mountainside. He and Killian were there hunting for her mom. Her Uncles had hired them to find their sister Ella Strong. Her mom took off down the mountain when someone tried to kidnap her. Storm was Frankie's bodyguard.

Frankie knew tears fell from her eyes. Her friend, Joy, kept wiping them away. She realized she was praying out loud when her nurses said Amen. She counted seven bullet holes. Three bullets were still in his body. Frankie had a lot of patching up to do when she raised her head for a second, she saw Jacob Burks. He winked at her. Frankie looked at the clock. Six hours had passed while she worked on Storm, and he was still breathing. His heart was beating. He was alive. She let Jacob take over while she stretched her body.

"They're out there waiting for you?"

"Who is?"

"The police. That idiot Hinkle said you risked a patient's life and went crazy. I know that's not true, right."

Frankie shrugged her shoulders, "I may have told him to fuck off a few times. The bastard pronounced Storm dead without even examining him. Just because he had all these bullet holes. If I hadn't heard Ash shouting for someone to help him. Storm would be dead right now. That fucker would have let him die. How many people has he let die?"

"I don't know. But I will watch Storm for you if you get arrested. I'm just saying, be prepared when you walk out of this room. I tried to make that idiot see what he was doing, but he wouldn't listen."

"That's okay because I'm going to the hospital board when this over. I want to see every patient's papers who has died that he's seen who has come in through the emergency room. He'll pay for not taking care of our patients."

"Frankie, don't say any of that when you go out there, or he'll make something up before you have a chance to say something."

"Jacob, promise me you won't let him anywhere around Storm. Joy, can you call his buddies. They'll guard his room. Their security business name is Band of Navy Seals. There might be some in the waiting room. Check there first."

"Okay, as soon as I finish here, I'll do that. What about when he's in ICU?"

"They have to stay with him always. Tell them what is going on. Do this before you call my Uncles?"

"Okay, you can count on me, Frankie."

"Thank you. Go do it now before I leave the operating room. We can finish here. Joy,

I want you to tell them I said Storm is going to make it. That's why I need them guarding him."

Joy nodded and walked out of the operating room. She walked down the hallway past the police waiting there to arrest Frankie. She walked to the waiting area, she opened the door, and stopped. The waiting room was full of people. Maybe there weren't that many. All of them were huge, like Frankie's Storm. She became a little tongue-tied looking at the handsome men.

"Do you have news for us about Storm lass?" A man with an Irish accent asked?

"Yes, Frankie said to tell you Storm is going to make it. But you have to guard him every second."

They all let out a breath and slapped each other on the back. "Why?" said the man with the beautiful Irish voice.

"Does someone want to harm him? Another asked.

"Damn, all of you get back. Hell, she can't breathe with you all standing over her."

Joy looked at the woman who walked in with coffee for everyone. She had the most beautiful gray eye Joy had ever seen. "Frankie is going to be arrested as soon as she comes out of the operating room. Your friends are already arrested. The police took them to jail. Doctor Hinkle called the police. He's angry because Frankie told him to…umm fuck off a few times. Because he pronounced Storm dead and became angry when Doctor Strong worked on Storm until his heart started beating again." Joy looked at them, "You should have seen it. We had to wipe the tears from Frankie's face. She was crying so hard, shouting for Storm's heart to beat. All of us nurses cried right along with her."

"Why does she think Storm needs a bodyguard?" Asked Irish, at least that's who Joy thought of him.

"Because Doctor Hinkle might do something if she's not

here to guard him. Frankie is going to file a complaint against him."

Killian looked at Kane, "Kane, you stay with him until I make a schedule."

Skye looked at Killian. "I'm going with him, I need to see Storm before I return home. My babies need their mommy."

"Can you take me to him now?" The handsome man said.

Joy now knew the Irish's guy's name was Kane. "I'll call and see if he's in the ICU." Joy picked up the phone and talked to the nurse's station. "He's in ICU. I'll point out Doctor Hinkle to you so you will know to keep him away from Storm. If you get a chance, take his picture and share it with your buddies."

Kane smiled, "You think like we do."

"My Dad was a detective for twenty-five years. Now he's retired and moved to Florida. I enjoyed talking to him about what case he was working on. It used to drive my mom crazy. I would have followed in his footsteps if Mom hadn't gotten so upset every time I mentioned it."

Killian waited for the cute nurse to take a breath from talking, "I'm going with you I want to see Storm before I leave. How many bullets did Storm have in him?"

"Seven, he came close to dying. But he had Frankie shouting at him, so he didn't dare die again. He died a few times, and she would yell at him while she brought him back to her. She must really love him. I've never heard about him before."

No one said a thing. So Joy figured she wouldn't learn anything from them. "Follow me, and I'll take you to Storm."

CHAPTER 2

Frankie watched Storm lying there. She felt his forehead, he felt a little warm, but his skin was always warm to the touch if she remembered correctly. Frankie touched his hand, and any other place she could touch that was uncovered. His hand twitched, and she felt it again. She saw his eyes open. He looked like he couldn't focus.

"Hey, Babe," he said, trying to focus on her. "I miss you." Then his eyes closed once again. He's done that a few times already. Frankie wondered if he even knew who he spoke with. Frankie smiled. She was so happy to hear that sexy voice say something. Those beautiful dark blue eyes were just a little unfocused. Her feelings for him hadn't diminished any. They only seemed to have intensified. *I love you Storm Anderson.*

~

Storm could feel someone staring at him even though he was still more asleep than awake. He opened his eyes. "Why is your ugly mug staring at me?"

Ash laughed out loud.

"I have to make sure you are still breathing. Or Frankie will have my hide."

"What has Frankie got to do with this? I can't believe I'm still living. I swear I died; I went to heaven…don't laugh. I did. My grandma was there, it was beautiful. The most peaceful feeling came over me. Now tell me, what the hell is going on?"

"First of all, you killed Geno so Willow can have peace in her and Ruby's life again. When we brought you in here, and the doctor in charge pronounced you dead. Frankie was here, and she heard us shouting. She saved your life, then got thrown in jail with Austin and me."

'What the fuck do you mean? Why did she get thrown in jail?"

"Let me finish telling the story. Frankie's Uncles bailed us out. She said you had to have a bodyguard in case Doctor Hinkle comes in here and kills you. He is the one who pronounced you dead. Frankie said she's going to make sure he loses his license. She is stirring up a beehive. I hope she knows what she's doing."

"How many bullets hit me?"

"Seven, three had to be taken out. From what Nurse Joy said, you died a few times in the operating room. Frankie would scream at you until she would get your heart beating again."

"What a mess. I don't want Frankie as my doctor."

"Why not?"

"Because I don't like her looking at my scars."

"Are you fucking kidding me? She cut your clothes off you. She's seen your body. How do you think she brought you back to life? Frankie operated on you. She took the bullets out. She doesn't give a fuck about your scars."

"I don't want to talk to her."

"I don't want to talk to you either, Storm, but I need to ask you some questions."

Storm knew he hurt her feelings. He saw it in her eyes. *Fuck. She was still as beautiful as he remembered. Her hair was longer, but it was still short. She grew her original blonde color. The last time he saw Frankie, it was red, and the curls framed her face. The curls were still there just longer.* Storm's eyes didn't move from hers. "Frankie, thank you for saving my life."

"Screw you." She said before she turned and walked out of the room.

Ash shook his head at his friend. "You are a dick. I swear, Storm, sometimes you say the stupidest things. I can't believe you did that. She saved your life after they told us you were dead. She was thrown into jail because she told the head of the hospital to fuck off numerous times. I saw how affected she was seeing you on that gurney without a heartbeat."

"Damn, I always screw things up when Frankie is involved. After Laura told me she didn't want to see my scars, it's something I couldn't shake off. I know Frankie isn't like that. I don't want to become involved with anyone. I'm not the faithful type."

"That's a damn lie. Laura my ass, you never loved Laura. Why are you doing this?"

"I can't talk anymore. I'm going to sleep."

"Fine. At least you know you'll be waking up because Frankie saved your life."

Storm kept his eyes shut, thinking about Frankie. He chuckled, remembering her wanting to switch places with him and Austin every other week. Storm knew he had to leave then, or he would be making love to her all night long, and she knew it. The way her hand lingered on his for longer than it needed to. The way Frankie cuddled up to him when he carried her outside to sit by the pool or anywhere else she needed to go. He wanted her, he ached for her, and she would become angry with him over the stupidest things. Frankie made him feel like an idiot when she told him to leave every other week. She wanted someone else for a bodyguard. After five times trading places with Austin and going to her Uncles, he decided he would go for good, so he traded places with Marc. Storm went to New York far enough away that Frankie couldn't call him back whenever she decided she wasn't upset with him anymore.

∼

Frankie went back later that evening after she knew Storm would be sleeping. His sleep was fitful. She could see the way pain crossed over his features. He moaned out loud. He was an ass. God, he could make her act like a child every time she was near him. No one had ever made her act the way she did when he was her bodyguard. She knew when she would have him trade places with Austin that it was stupid. It was either that, or she would have her way with him and beg him to make love to her. In all her thirty-three-years, she has never wanted anyone the way she wanted Storm. The feelings never left her. It's been two years, and she still wanted him as much as she did then. When she saw him lying on that gurney, she couldn't breathe. She heard Hinkle say he was dead, and she admits she went a little crazy. But she loved him. Frankie has loved him since he carried her to the helicopter on that mountainside. Frankie would never admit she loved him out loud. Only to herself would she admit that unfortunate truth.

When Storm was her bodyguard, Frankie wanted Storm to throw her on the bed and make passionate love to her. She hinted enough times, but he ignored all her hints. When he went to New York, it broke her heart. She trusted him to keep her safe from the person who tried to kidnap her mom. And she missed him so much she would cry herself to sleep until she gave herself a good talking to. She was a grown woman acting like a sixteen-year-old teenager with her first crush.

Marc nodded his head when she walked into the room. Frankie checked to see the drips were working correctly and stood at the foot of the bed pretending to read the information on the clipboard. She just had to see for herself he was okay.

Frankie didn't notice Storm watched her. She didn't look at Storm while Marc was there.

"Give us a minute Marc." Storm said, looking at Frankie. Marc walked to stand on the outside of the door. "Hey, Babe, come over here, pull up that chair." Storm said, trying to hold up his hand with all the IVs in it. She didn't move. She stood in the same spot. "Frankie, I'm sorry I'm an ass. I have no explanation for my rudeness. I'm a little pissed that I was shot, and I'm sorry, I don't mean to treat you like I did. I guess I'm still angry from before."

"What do you mean from before?"

"From when you kept sending me away."

"I didn't send you to New York."

"No, but every time I went to your Uncles to switch places with Austin, I had to face their laughter and their friendly jabs. It was becoming embarrassing. So I decided to leave once and for all. That way, you wouldn't get angry at me anymore."

"That's bullshit, and you know it. The only reason you left was because I made it evident to you that I wanted you to make love to me. You were scared to get into a relationship with me."

"What the hell are you talking about? I swear to God, Frankie, why do you always want to argue with me? Babe, I don't want to argue. I owe you my life."

"You don't owe me anything. I came here to tell you I have to be out of the country for a while. Jacob Burks will take over for me. I hope you don't have any difficulties. Take care of yourself Storm, your life is very precious, and you have to take care of it. Goodbye."

"Please wait. It's hard for me to explain myself. I'm not like the others who have an easy way with words. I left because I knew if I didn't go, we would have ended up in bed together. I didn't want to hurt you. I wanted you, I still want you, but you would have ended up getting hurt and hating me."

"Why didn't you let me decide for myself if I would have allowed you to make love to me?"

"I know you would have. You wanted me as much as I wanted you. I recognized all the signals, and when I didn't act on those signals, you would become angry and send me to trade places with Austin. I worked for your uncles. I wasn't about to take advantage of their niece. No, matter how hard it was staying away from you." Storm could have kicked himself for telling her all of that. His head hurt, and he felt like he was going to vomit. He heaved, and his body hurt like hell. He felt like someone beat him with a bat. His body hurt so badly. He looked at Frankie, and she shouted for the nurse.

"I'm going to get you something for the pain. I'm sorry for upsetting you. What is wrong with me? I swear I have never argued with anyone else, only you."

She was busy setting him up with another drip and didn't notice him looking at her. If Frankie had looked up, she would have seen the look in his eyes. He felt more for her than just wanting to make love to her. He wished he could be with Frankie, but they were nothing alike. Storm had a rough life. If it wasn't for his grandma, he would have been all alone living on the streets with his drug addict mother. When a policeman found him sleeping under a bench when he was eight, he asked Storm if he had a family. Storm didn't know he had a grandma until they found his mom, and she told them he had a grandma. From that night on, he lived with his grandma. Frankie deserved someone who had the same background as she did.

Frankie raised her eyes to his. "I'm sorry. What kind of doctor am I to cause my patient to be in pain? Please forgive me."

"Frankie, you are the best doctor I've ever met. You have nothing to apologize for. It's my own fault. For bringing it all up again."

"I can see you're getting tired. I'll have the nurse give you something to help you sleep." She turned and walked out of the room.

CHAPTER 3

Storm ran alongside Ash. They ran in the mountains out of Los Angeles. It's been three months since he got out of the hospital, and he hadn't seen or heard anything from Frankie. He needed to thank her properly. He felt like a piece of crap for the way he talked to her. He wanted to apologize. He needed to see her. Why the hell is she still out of the country? He guessed he would have to go talk to her Uncles and see if they've heard from her. He looked over at Ash, "Let's stop by the McKenna ranch and see if Shane or one of the guys have heard from Frankie."

"Why are you looking for Frankie?"

"I need to thank her for saving my life. Plus, I need to apologize for the way I acted towards her. Jacob Burks said she hasn't been back to the States since I was in the hospital."

"Yeah, that's a long time to stay in another country. I don't mind stopping by the ranch. I'm sure Frankie is somewhere in the State's."

"She isn't answering her phone."

"Maybe she doesn't want to talk to you."

"Yeah, that could be true. I still want to stop by there."

Storm ran up the last mountain and climbed into the truck. They weren't that far from the McKenna ranch. It was outside of the city. Storm pulled onto the long driveway and noticed the horses were standing outside of the front door. "I've never seen horses let loose like this before on the ranch. They always are where they're supposed to be, in the corral or the barn. These two still have the saddles on them."

Storm and Ash walked up to the large front door and knocked. They looked at each other when they heard shouting from inside. "I wonder what's wrong. It sounds like they are fixing to get into a fist fight." He knocked again, but the shouting became louder. "Fuck it," He opened the door and walked inside. The brothers were in a huge argument. "Shut the hell up. Why are you three fighting?"

"What are you doing here?" Shane looked at his brother's. "We weren't supposed to call anyone."

"We didn't call anyone. Why are you two here?" James, the oldest brother, demanded. Even though they were Frankie's uncles, they were the ages of Storm and his buddies. Their father married their mother when Ella Frankie's mom was fifteen-years-old.

Storm stood with his legs slightly apart. If he had to beat the truth out of these three, he would. They were hiding something. "What the hell is wrong?"

"Why do you think something is wrong?"

"Because your horses are walking around in your driveway."

"Fuck," James said as he took the phone and told a ranch hand to put the horses away.

"Tell me," Storm growled. He felt in his heart it had to do with Frankie.

"Someone has Frankie," Shane exclaimed out loud.

"Damn it, Shane, shut the fuck up," Trey demanded.

"You might as well spill it. You've told us this much." Ash said, looking at the three brothers.

James ran his hand through his blonde hair. It looked like he'd done that a few hundred times. "We're waiting for another call from Frankie. We were getting worried because she was supposed to be home two weeks ago. I flew over to Saudi Arabia, but I couldn't find her anywhere. I went to the hospital, and they said she left there three weeks ago. I flew home thinking we must have missed each other on the flights. We haven't talked to her in three weeks. That is not like Frankie. Our sister Ella is ready to start a war to get her daughter back. She thinks someone is holding Frankie against her will. Ella has gone to Capitol Hill to fight for her daughter. Today Frankie called, Rosa answered she told her she couldn't talk. She was afraid of being overheard. Rosa had someone hunt us down. We are hoping she will call back. Whoever has her must have taken her phone away."

Storm walked over to the French door and looked out at the mountains. "So she called and let you know she was alive. I believe your sister is right. Someone is holding Frankie against her will." Storm shook his head. He felt like hitting something. "When I get my hands on that bastard, I will kill him," he roared at the top of his voice.

"I told you he loved her," Shane said, looking at his brothers. "We'll hire the Seals to find Frankie, but I'm going with you guys to bring her back."

"Hold up there, Shane. We need to talk about this. We have to wait until we hear from Frankie. We don't know where she is. Or who has her? She told Rosa she would call back as soon as she has a chance."

"I don't give a damn if you hire us or not; I'm going after Frankie," Storm looked at Shane, "I am not in love with Frankie. I owe her my life, and she's my friend. Don't make more out of this than what it is."

Shane looked over at Ash, who shrugged his shoulders. He thought like Shane did, but kept it to himself. When Storm admits to himself, he loves Frankie, then Ash would tell him everyone already knew it. Until then, he refused to discuss it with anyone.

Storm looked at Ash, "Do you want to call Killian and tell him what is going on? I'm not leaving this house until we hear from Frankie."

"Yeah, I'll give him a call."

Storm walked towards the kitchen, "I'm putting a pot of coffee on."

"I've already put the coffee on Mr. Storm. You go back and wait by the phone."

"Thank you, Rosa. I'll have my coffee black." Storm watched the brothers arguing. He got along with these men. They ran one of the largest horse ranches in the country and were considered the three most eligible bachelors in the country. Being billionaires didn't hurt either. Storm had to admit they didn't act any different than their workers. He knew they worked as hard as the men who worked for them. He worked alongside of them when he was at their home guarding their sister Ella and their niece Frankie.

It was three in the morning when the phone rang. Trey grabbed it up on the first ring. "Where are you?"

"I'm not sure," Frankie whispered.

"What do you mean you're not sure?"

"Give me the damn phone," Storm said, taking the phone from Trey. "Tell me what happened."

"Storm, what are you doing there?"

"I came here to find out where you were. Let's focus on you. Tell me what happened?"

"Don't start an argument with me."

Storm smiled and shook his head. "Frankie, focus."

"I was in the airport. I saw this Sheik and his men walk

by. He stopped and looked at me. The next thing I knew, an airport guard told me I had to answer some questions. They said I had drugs and was being arrested. I told them they were wrong, I said I didn't have anything, that I came to their country to perform surgery on three children. The next thing I know, some men walk into the room and start talking to the airport officials. Then they are pushing me out the door and into a black vehicle, and I'm being driven for an hour out of the city. No one would talk to me. The doors were locked, and I couldn't get out of the vehicle."

"Do you know the guy's name?"

"I don't know anything. I've been here for two weeks, and this is the first day I ventured out of where they put me. There are lots of women here, and I think they all belong to the Sheik. I have to get out of here before he adds me to his list of women."

"Damn, what country are you in?"

"Saudi Arabia. I have to go. I don't want anyone to catch me on the phone. Tell my Uncles to come after me."

"Oh, don't you worry, we'll come after you and that Sheik will regret taking you."

"I'll look forward to meeting you." A male voice said before the phone went dead.

Storm looked at the phone. "The Sheik heard every word we said. He said he looks forward to meeting us. He knew Frankie would use the phone the first chance she got." Storm took out his phone and called Killian. "The Sheik overheard us talking to Frankie. He knows we're going after her. She's in Saudi Arabia."

"Do you know who took her?"

"No, we don't know where she is. We'll get the truth out of the men who work at the airport. They are the ones responsible for her being taken."

"I have the plane ready. Kane is going with us. He speaks their language."

"We'll meet you at the airport. Grab mine and Ash's bags." Storm looked at the brothers, "Who's going with us?"

"We are all going." James said, "let us pack a few things."

Printed in Great Britain
by Amazon